Shelf Life of Happiness

Shelf Life of Happiness

Stories by Virginia Pye

Press 53

Winston-Salem

Press 53, LLC
PO Box 30314
Winston-Salem, NC 27130

First Edition

Cover design by Margaret Buchanan
www.buchanandesign.net

Author photo by Tennessee Photographs
www.tennesseephotographs.com

Library of Congress Control Number
2018943331

Printed on acid-free paper
978-1-941209-82-0

For Eva and Daniel

Happiness makes up in height what it lacks in length.
—Robert Frost

Now and then it's good to pause in our pursuit of happiness and just be happy.
—Guillaume Appollinaire

CONTENTS

Best Man

Snow fell hard up in Reno. The interstate started out gray, but as the elevation rose, the white line disappeared and cars crawled as they came into town. Keith gently pressed his foot against the floorboard in sympathy with Caroline, who was at the wheel and making slow, intermittent progress behind a snowplow that scattered wet sand. It struck the windshield and made a sound like rice hitting the backs of a bride and groom.

Keith had arrived in San Francisco on a flight from New York that afternoon. He was here to serve as best man to his closest friend Don, who planned to marry his new girlfriend Caroline up in Reno on this Wednesday afternoon. No one had expected a surprise late-April storm and Keith wondered if that might change things. From the passenger seat, he handed Caroline a bandanna, which she used to wipe the fogging glass.

The car heater whirred on high to keep Don warm in the back seat. He was fast asleep and snoring, a sleeping bag bundled up to his chin. Keith remembered that familiar sound from their tiny freshman dorm room where their beds had been so close he could reach across and poke Don to get him to stop. Keith was tempted to

do that now, but when he looked around, the sight of
Don made him suck in air between his teeth. Keith's old
friend looked worse than bad, even when sleeping, or
maybe especially when sleeping.

Caroline spoke softly. "He wants his ashes tossed out
over the ocean."

Keith nodded as if he were prepared for this. He had
met Caroline for the first time at the airport only a few
hours before and assumed they'd skirt the issue for at
least a little while longer.

"He wants you and your old buddies to toss them into
the ocean off Cape Cod."

"Sure," Keith said.

He couldn't imagine it, couldn't fathom it—how Don
had arrived so suddenly at the end of his life. As the wipers
did their hypnotic best with the wet snow, Keith looked
at Caroline's striking profile and tried to piece things
together. A half year earlier, this petite, athletic-looking
woman had moved in with Don when he could no longer
take care of himself. Don hadn't bothered to mention
over the phone that she was a beauty, though he did
call her a dynamo and someone to be reckoned with,
which Don said he needed. She had taken over caring
for him with intense, though loving, determination.
Based on what Don had said, Keith had pictured
someone more masculine, a hardy nurse-type, not this
fine-boned woman with the blond ponytail and
Pacific-blue eyes.

The even harder part to figure was that three months
before that, Don had seemed perfectly well. In August,
Keith and Don had done wind sprints on the beach in
Wellfleet with their college friends. Maybe Don had been
slower than he used to be, but none of them were getting
any younger. By the bonfire, Don had brought out an
African drum and everyone danced. He'd just gotten back

from two years in Swaziland with the Peace Corps. Keith
had no reason to believe Don was anything but fine.

That fall, Keith had flipped past occasional *Times*
articles about the new gay illness, worse than cancer. Then
Don said the word AIDS over the phone and Keith started
seeing it everywhere. From what Keith gathered, Don's
treatments were experimental, complex, and highly
ineffectual. He looked like shit and had said point-blank
he wouldn't be around for long. The snowplow's chains
scraped rhythmically now like the drum made out of a
gourd and seeds that Don liked to play, his head tossed
back and his mouth open. That was the Don Keith knew.

"He's got his funeral all figured out," Caroline said.
"Typical, meticulous Don."

"You guys talk like that? I mean, about afterwards?"

"It reassures him to know things will go on without
him." Caroline turned the car into a parking lot. "I guess
it helps him feel ready."

She adjusted the rearview mirror so she could see Don
sleeping in the backseat. "We're here, love," she said in a
louder voice. "The Silver Bells, just like we planned it."

Don shifted and grumbled. The sleeping bag rustled a
little, and then suddenly more, as he started to fight it,
his arms caught in the slick fabric, his eyes still shut. Keith
reached back and tried to pull the bag down Don's chest,
but in half-sleep, Don knocked him away and kept
thrashing.

"Keith's here, honey," Caroline said. "Time to wake up."

At these words, Don finally stopped struggling and
the bag slipped down from around his chest to make a
forlorn puddle at his waist. His eyes flicked open and,
although Keith searched in them for signs of pain, or
suffering, or sadness, a wide smile appeared across his
friend's too-thin face.

"Fuck you guys," Don said with a happy lilt.

"Hey, man," Keith said and reached to squeeze his friend's bony knee. "Time to rise and shine. You're getting married."

Pink neon flashed through the thick snowfall—two hearts, two bells, alternating over the parking lot. Caroline had pulled her Corolla next to a rusted Cadillac, the only car left outside the cement-block building.

"Looks like a porno shop," Keith said.

Don cocked an eyebrow. "How perfect is that?"

Caroline turned off the car engine.

"All right, let's go," Keith said and didn't hesitate as he climbed out.

The door slammed behind him with a muffled echo. It took him a moment to notice that he hovered alone in the quiet as snow accumulated quickly on his shoulders. Overheated and headachy from the long drive, he welcomed the biting wind. He peered back into the car and remembered that, of course, Don couldn't move fast. His friend was an invalid now. It would drive Keith crazy to go so slowly all the time. It would have driven the old Don crazy, too. It didn't seem to bother Caroline, though. She had the patience of, what?—Keith drew a swirl through the snow landing on the hood—an angel. He scattered the snow with his open palm.

Keith peered through the fogged window again and watched as Caroline reached back to unbuckle Don. But then, to Keith's surprise, Don slapped her hand away, and not in a gentle or kidding fashion. He lashed out several times, but Caroline's voice retaliated just as firmly. It cut through the glass of the window and the hush of the snow. She was a teacher scolding a naughty kid, her voice controlled and calm, yet full of purpose.

"I'm not taking any bullshit from you," she said. "This was your idea and I'm with you, but you've got to control yourself. It's the fucking drugs. Just try not to be a pain in the ass today."

Keith blew warm breath on his fingers and wondered how Caroline managed, how they both managed. Don had never been an angel, and apparently now that was truer than ever. Keith stomped the snow off his boots and felt something like embarrassment at the strength of his own sturdy legs.

Caroline climbed out of the car and shut her door. "Your turn," she said.

"Sure, I'll get him," Keith said, but then paused. "Hey, you OK?"

Caroline sighed. "I'm fine. I'm the fucking bride."

And although she said it with a smirk, in that moment she looked like a bride to Keith. She tipped her head back, exposing a white throat, and tried to catch snowflakes on her tongue. He realized how young she was. Seven, maybe even ten years younger than Don and he. She wasn't shivering, but seemed to be vibrating with cold, or trepidation, or even excitement. Where the snow fell on her neck, the skin turned instantly pink. She let out a long breath and then walked around and fiddled with her keys to open the back of the station wagon.

Keith could see why Don had fallen for her, though his friend had been only into guys since early in their college years. It seemed weirdly out of character for Don to revert back to dating a woman after getting into the whole gay scene out in California. Keith himself would have fallen for Caroline in a heartbeat, had circumstances been different. She was exactly his type. That must have occurred to Don, Keith thought. It almost made him wonder if his friend was marrying someone just to show him how it was done. Keith realized that was a pretty screwed-up idea—as if Don was living his life for Keith's benefit. They were close, closer than any other friend or girlfriend Keith had ever had, but that didn't mean Don would marry someone for his sake. Still, Keith thought it strange that Don had had no interest in women, except for this particular one.

"Found it," she called from the back of the car as she held up a manila envelope. "The marriage license."

Keith joined her and gathered the dozen roses he'd bought at the airport. He presented them to her without show. Caroline stood on tiptoes and kissed his cold cheek.

Once inside the Silver Bells, the flowers looked limp and bitten by cold, but the wife of the Justice of the Peace complimented Caroline on them anyway. When she offered Caroline a hand mirror and a comb and encouraged her to freshen up, Caroline declined. She shook out her hair and snow flew off and onto the back of Keith's hand where it quickly melted.

Caroline whispered to him, "My mamma treated me like I was a baby doll when I was little. I had this white-blond hair and dark eyelashes and I think she wanted to make some money off of me. But I put up such a stink, she finally gave up, though I suppose I was pretty cute."

"I bet," Keith said.

He wasn't sure what she was hinting at as she swayed before him. She had to know she was beautiful. But as Keith wondered if she was flirting with him, she turned to Don in his wheelchair and said, "But beauty's in the eye of the beholder, isn't it, my love?" She bent down and kissed the hollow of Don's cheek.

He chuckled and looked up at Keith. "Caroline has a hell of an imagination. She still thinks I'm handsome."

Keith tried to see the handsomeness she saw in Don, but he almost hated to look at his old friend, he was so changed.

The Justice of the Peace then called the three in and they lined up before him. His wife played an abbreviated version of Pachelbel's Canon on an electronic keyboard and the official read a brief version of the ceremony from a card he had long ago memorized. When he pronounced them husband and wife, Don let go of Keith's coat sleeve and Caroline bent down so he could kiss her on the lips. Keith noticed the wife of the Justice staring at Don. You'd have to be blind not to guess he didn't have long. Don let out a long, shallow sigh that worried Keith. In this happy moment, he tried not to hear his friend's labored breathing.

Keith stepped out of the 7-Eleven and turned up the collar of his parka before starting the trek back across the parking lot to the motel. In a plastic bag, he carried a six pack of beer, three submarine sandwiches, some chips, a deck of cards, and, as wedding gifts, an *I'd Rather Be in Reno* cap for Don, and a bottle of bath beads for Caroline. He knew he was getting off cheap and decided to insist on paying for the room.

As he ducked into the wind, he heard a woman's voice calling out to him. "Hey, don't forget your change."

He turned back to see the cashier, a college girl with black lipstick and even blacker hair. She stood shivering at the door of the store.

"Sorry," Keith said and trotted back to her.

She tucked a strand of hair behind one ear. "You just passing through?" she asked.

Keith pointed with a gloveless hand toward the motel. "Home away from home."

"Good thing you got in before the storm. They shut down the roads an hour ago. State trooper stopped by and said he'd drive me home if I wanted."

Her black lipstick was cracked at the edges and her cheeks were marked by a sharp runway of rouge, just asking to be smudged off. Keith wanted to lean in and use his tongue to do it, but instead he said, "Lucky guy."

The girl blushed.

Keith realized he was doing it again, doing that thing that came too easily for him. His arms hung loose at his sides, his head dipped lower, and he looked right at her. The girl tucked her hair again.

"Looks like I'm closing early. We've got VHS tapes in the back and an eight track, you know, to dance. You should come by."

Keith bobbed and stuffed one hand into the front pocket of his jeans. "What about the trooper?"

"Screw him," she said and tried to laugh. "So see you later?"

"Later," he said and turned into the driving snow as he headed across the parking lot again.

If Don had been there with him and it was back in college, they'd have stayed around just to see what might happen next. Don didn't care about the girls. He'd fool around with them, but he was mostly there to keep an eye on Keith, both egging him on and making sure he didn't get into too much trouble. Keith had an uncanny way with women, which Don didn't seem to mind one bit. If anything, what bothered Don was that Keith, while drowning in the possibility of love, stayed afloat. Don hated how Keith kept his heart in reserve. But Keith was sure he'd open up eventually. He just hadn't met the right girl yet. But now, more than a decade later, he had to wonder. He'd had only a string of short relationships to show for all his good luck. He was at Don's wedding after all and not the other way around.

He made it back to the motel and slumped against the door to the room before opening it, the exhaustion from his travels getting to him. He shut his eyes and an image of Caroline with her head tipped back, her tongue catching snow, appeared under his eyelids. She was so young and vibrant, Keith could feel the blood coursing through the vein at his temple where it pressed against the doorjamb. In that moment, he felt he had too much blood—too much good, healthy blood. The image of his best friend's bride swirled before him, her arms outstretched, teasing him with her grace. Keith opened his eyes with a start, straightened up, and fumbled for the room key.

In the darkened room, Don curled under a mountain of covers on the far bed. Caroline rose from where she'd been sitting beside him as he slept. Keith wondered if she had been watching over Don the whole time he was gone—just bent there, stroking his head, as gentle as that.

She patted Keith's chest to welcome him back and said, "All right, let's eat. I'm starved."

"You think he's hungry?" Keith asked.

"No, we'll let him rest."

Keith tossed his wet coat onto the carpet by the door and took off his boots. Caroline unpacked the food and tore the Reno tourist magazine in two for plates. They sat by the window while the snow outside came down like snow in a globe—persistent, fake, and yet perfect. Keith opened two beers and brought them over.

"I ought to propose a toast to you guys." He raised his bottle, but only half-heartedly. How could you celebrate a wedding like this one?

Caroline lifted her beer but then set it down again, clearly exhausted. "Not exactly the wedding a girl pictures growing up," she said. "My mamma always wanted the whole shebang for me."

Keith drank his beer and didn't know what to say.

"She knows we're doing this," Caroline continued. "Since meeting Don, she hasn't complained, not even once. He can be such a charmer. I think she's just happy I'm with a guy."

The beer burned the back of Keith's throat, as he tried to guess what she meant.

"What, Don didn't tell you?" Caroline asked, leaning toward him.

Keith shrugged.

"Don's funny about things like that. He likes to keep secrets. He really doesn't have to, but he does anyway. Everything's so obvious."

Nothing seemed obvious to Keith, and he wanted to ask more.

Caroline got up and went to the thermostat. She turned it up all the way and hot air blasted out of the vents. "Sorry about the heat. He's like a hothouse flower now."

She unzipped her jeans and shimmied out of them, then stood without embarrassment in a pair of boxer shorts that probably belonged to Don. She next pulled off her sweater and t-shirt, leaving only a tank top. Keith felt his breastbone ache.

Caroline went over to Don, who remained unmoving under the pile of blankets. She pulled them higher to his chin and he shifted in his sleep. She bent over and kissed his pale forehead, then settled down opposite Keith at the small table again.

"He's *this* sick and still so sweet," she said.

Keith had never thought of Don as sweet. He wasn't sweet. That was one of the things Keith liked about him.

"I guess we're still in the honeymoon phase," Caroline said, and took a bite of her sandwich. "You must think I don't know him very well."

Keith set down his beer and leaned back. "No, you know him." He liked how she assumed he knew Don better, which was true. With Don's previous relationships—the dramatic in-love times and the heartbreak times—Keith had seen his friend through it all.

"Were you surprised when he told you he was getting hitched to a woman? Come on, tell me the truth."

Keith let out a quick laugh. "Well, yeah. He used to

say he never wanted to tie another person down, especially not himself. And girls never were his thing."

She gazed out the window for a long moment, then shrugged and took a bite. Through the chewing, she started talking. "He sort of regrets all that now. Not being gay, but he wishes he'd been more honest, you know, in showing who he *really* loved. He hid it too much of the time. But then he decided he didn't want us to stay secret anymore, because I'd been like that, too, never really committing myself to anyone. It was time for me, and for Don, and for you, too, I gather. At least that's what Don thinks."

Keith stared at her hard, her lovely profile burning into him. What was she saying to him, about Don, and himself, and her? He noticed his heart had started beating faster. Too much blood coursed through him again, as he felt his pulse throb in his neck. Who *had* Don loved? Keith wanted to ask outright, but was afraid of the answer she might give, or even of the fact that she might have an answer at all.

Keith sat up and crumpled the greasy deli paper. She had no business knowing about him and Don. That was their private business, their friendship that went back to when they were not yet men. But if she did know things about him, Keith realized that meant Don had told her recently. Don had been thinking of Keith right when Keith was all the way across the country and thinking of Don. The whole thing felt like a tangle, one Keith needed urgently to understand before it was too late and Don was gone.

"They say getting sick can change a person," Caroline added, taking a swig of beer.

She seemed so casual, as if talking this way were just the easiest thing in the world. Keith tried to frame a question that might reveal what he wanted to know, but the words didn't come and he wondered if words were the wrong thing anyway.

Don rolled onto his side just then and his eyelashes flickered open. Keith rose and went and sat on the edge of the second bed. He leaned across the space toward his old friend.

"Hey, man, how you feeling?" he asked.

Don smiled faintly.

Keith looked down at the peeling skin on Don's forehead and lips. His cheekbones protruded, his eyes far too deep, as if a face could be melted down to the skull and still be called a face. Keith wanted to reach out and touch the dry, cracking surface of him. Don was turning to ashes already. Soon Keith and their friends would scatter him over the ocean.

Keith's eyes stung and he dabbed at them with pinched fingers that came up damp. He knew he'd cry. He already had, standing at his kitchen sink in Brooklyn, on the subway one time, then on the plane, and now here. It didn't matter to him that people saw, especially not Caroline, who seemed to know how much he and Don had gone through together. Still, he didn't move closer. He didn't reach out to touch his friend, rub his shoulders, or touch his hand. Then Don shut his eyes again.

Caroline slipped in beside Keith on the second bed and they both watched as Don's breath grew steady and he drifted off to sleep again.

"He was scared he wouldn't get to see you," she whispered. "It's so amazing you're here," she squeezed Keith's knee. "Now he can finally relax. He used to wake up in the night with panic attacks and call out your name. The meds can do that."

Caroline bent down and unloaded prescription bottles from a medical bag, lining them up on the bedside table. Then she crouched on the carpet, looking for an outlet for the oxygen machine. Keith knew he should help her. He should do or say something, but he couldn't take his eyes off her breasts as they jiggled under her thin undershirt, and his mind was stuck on one burning thought: Don had called out his name in the night?

Caroline got the machine working and turned up the dials, expertly placing the mask over Don's face without waking him. She sat beside Keith again and whispered, "That's pretty typical, by the way. The night sweats and delusions. I've had to pretend I was you more than once just to get him to calm down. Then it passes and the old Don comes back."

Keith looked from her to Don. His friend's eyelids were red and riddled with thin, blue veins. The old Don? What did she know of the old Don? Keith suddenly couldn't stand the thought of her pretending to be him, as if his friendship with Don could be faked by someone else. He knew that wasn't what she meant, but somehow it still bothered him that she had held Don when he had called out Keith's name. He should have been there.

Don's eyes slowly opened again. It seemed to take him a moment to remember where he was. He stared at Keith with great intensity and Keith wondered if perhaps his friend was still dreaming. Was that possible? Or was he confusing it with how people looked when they died and their eyes remained open? It took Don forever to blink and Keith felt the panic rising in him as he worried that he was losing him in that long moment.

"You're here," Don said, his voice muffled behind the rubber mask.

"I am."

"You hear I got married?"

"Sure enough," Keith said. "I'm your best man."

"Always were," Don said.

Keith felt the tears rise up fast. Neither Don nor

Caroline seemed to notice them rolling down his cheeks, or if they did, it must have seemed so natural to them and routine, they didn't comment.

"I don't deserve her, you know," Don said, "You of all people know that I don't."

Keith wanted Don to keep talking about how he of all people knew Don best, but he realized he was supposed to be polite and say something nice about Caroline. Instead, all he could muster was, "Of course you do."

He reached across and squeezed the blankets, barely finding the thin rail of Don's arm beneath. He thought he saw in Don's eyes a flicker of his former mischief, a roughness and playfulness that no longer suited him and was snuffed out quickly by a passing jolt of pain. But for a moment, the old Don was back, flirting, making light of something as complex and unspeakable as love.

"How you feeling, darling?" Caroline asked and shifted closer.

Don's face and body relaxed at the sound of her voice. With effort, he pulled his arm out from under the blanket and reached for her hand. Keith moved aside to let her slip in and, as he did so, he let himself realize that, for whatever reasons that made sense only to the bride and groom, it was right. She smoothed Don's brow and little flecks of skin fell onto the pillow. Keith stood and turned to the window. It was too hot in the room, too close. He realized he couldn't stand to stay much longer.

Caroline opened the prescription bottles and poured pills onto her open palm. "Keith brought us some cards for poker," she said in that loud voice she used with Don. His friend's hearing must be shot, too, Keith realized. And hadn't Don said something about his eyesight going as well? There was hardly anything left of him.

Don's voice came out soft, but clear. "Deal me in. I'm going clean you both out. Tonight's my honeymoon."

Keith went back to the bed where the couple huddled. He wanted to make a joke of it, or be jovial, offering lightness and life to the occasion, but his head ached and he needed air and he thought he might start crying again if he said anything to Don. He decided he would play a few hands. Drink the rest of the beer. Then, when his old friend had fallen asleep again, he'd head over to the 7-Eleven to see what kind of trouble he could get himself into.

The door to the convenience store was locked and the lights turned off. Keith pressed his nose to the glass. He thought he saw movement from under the door of a back room, so he started pounding the glass with his fist. It made a muffled, ineffectual thud as the snow fell thicker, subduing everything. He and the college girl would watch a flick, drink some beer, screw around, and soon, Keith hoped, he would remember who he was.

Being around Don had always been confusing. Near the end of college, when Don came out, Keith had gotten nervous and tried to keep his distance. He didn't want Don getting the wrong idea about him, although they'd been best friends for years by then. It seemed silly now, but at the time, he thought maybe Don's roving eye would land on him. It hadn't, and Don had been nothing but patient with Keith until he relaxed and they went back to being friends.

Keith finally stopped pounding and leaned his back against the store window. He watched the snow fall into the triangles of streetlight. The sky was white although it was night and the streetlight was white, too, the same as the sky. It would have torn him up to be with the college girl, although it pained him not to be with her, too.

He pushed off from the glass, dug his chafed hands into the pockets of his jeans and pressed into the wind. Snow rose to the tops of his work boots as he headed up the road, past strip malls with darkened beauty parlors and pizza joints with their neon signs shut off. He stopped under a traffic light that swung back and forth roughly in the wind. He noticed the tears only when they slipped down his collar.

He thought about Don after college, when he acted wild and free and was screwing around with anyone he liked. After he'd left for the West Coast, Don would call Keith in the middle of the night to tell him about the guy he'd become infatuated with that week. The man who had made his heart sing, but then quickly broke it. Every time, Keith had offered the same hard-boiled advice: Don needed to put up his guard and protect himself better. Keith let out a sad grunt at the irony of that phrase now. Don had not heeded his advice even once, and yet never seemed to regret it, although look where that had gotten him.

Keith swiped the tears with his jacket sleeve, but that only made his face wetter and colder with the melted snow. He had tried to convince himself that he was like Don, too—screwing around with girls just for the hell of it. But the truth was, although he sometimes acted the same as his friend, he remained aloof. He waited— though for what or whom he didn't know. He hid his heart far more than ever revealing it, even to himself. Keith was the one with secrets and look where that had gotten him, too.

He turned back and pressed through the falling snow. When he finally reached the motel room door, his fingers were so cold he could barely hold the key. This time it wasn't jet lag that made him weak. Keith couldn't stop thinking about the moment Caroline and Don had kissed at the end of the marriage service. Don had let out a sigh as he and his new wife pulled away from one another. It worried Keith at the time, but now he realized it had been a sigh of contentment. Don had found love, with Caroline and any number of other times before that in his life.

The blast of warm air made Keith's eyes sting. He shut the door softly and stood shivering, his teeth chattering, hands and feet so cold they burned. On the far bed, Don lay under the mound of blankets. Caroline, in her thin tank top and shorts, lay on top of the covers and spooned against him. Her eyes were shut. Don's breathing was noisy and labored, but steady.

It took Keith's icy fingers a while to work the buttons of his coat and unlace his boots. His jeans folded stiffly where he dropped them. He stripped out of his clothes and tiptoed to his pack, crouched down, and fumbled for dry clothing. When Caroline shifted on the bed and opened her eyes, Keith went still and stopped breathing. He sensed he was waiting for something, only he didn't know what.

With a long, graceful arm, Caroline patted the bed behind her back. It took Keith a moment to understand. Then he let his shirt fall to the carpet and walked over. He slipped onto the bed as gently as he could and lay down beside her. Caroline didn't turn to see him, but adjusted her hips so he would scoot forward and spoon against her back.

A moment later, she startled him even more. She stretched her top leg, pointing her toes, and draped it over his, laughing a little under her breath and shifting closer. She snuggled her back against his cold chest and it made his whole body shiver. The tips of her hair brushed against his dry lips and tickled his wind-slapped cheeks.

As she shifted and shimmied, getting comfortable before going still again, Keith thought his chest might explode with the beating of his heart. He could barely keep himself from grabbing her, kissing her, pressing himself against her, even screwing her, as wild and unlikely and plain wrong as that seemed. But he couldn't stop thinking about Don, too. How could he not, with his friend so close and breathing in such a difficult way?

Poor, brittle Don, who had nothing left to give after all those years of giving to everyone. Then Caroline interrupted Keith's thoughts by reaching behind her back and taking his wrist. He wanted so badly for her to bring his hand up and across her body to caress her breast. He wanted her to lean back into him so he could kiss the hot place under her hair. Instead, she lifted his arm and draped it across her ribs, placing Keith's palm not on her own breast, but under the covers and onto Don's bare, narrow chest. She rested it there carefully, as if not to bruise either man.

Keith's breath caught and he thought he had never felt anything so tender as his sleeping friend's skin. Don's chest rose and fell and Keith tried to focus on each intake and exhale. He tried to forget about Caroline, her body humming with life as it pressed up against him. But there was no escaping her, and Keith couldn't, didn't want to. She finally turned her head toward him, whispered something, and then leaned her face even closer and kissed him on the lips.

In his hot brain and cold body, Keith felt everything at once. He couldn't stand the thought of waiting any longer. They kissed and kissed again and didn't stop. Then Caroline pulled back and smiled and did something that really frightened him. She shifted away and turned to her new husband and kissed him hard enough on the lips to wake him. As Don's eyes opened, Keith prepared to slip off the bed and stand. He would put on his clothes and get going again, grab his bag and head out the door, though to where he wasn't sure. He just knew he couldn't stay a moment longer if he had ruined everything with his old friend.

But when Don's eyes finally focused on Keith's face, he didn't look angry or even surprised that his best man lay pressed up against his bride's back, his arm draped over her naked side. Instead, Don nodded ever so slightly, and the edges of his gray, dry lips started to rise. Yes, Don's eyes were shining and that mischievous look had returned, the one that Keith had tried so long to dismiss or correct. But now, he wondered if he had misunderstood their meaning all along: Don wasn't conveying something as slight as mischief, but instead, a larger thing, like love.

Caroline had seen the look in Don's eyes, too, and she, being more like Don than Keith would ever be, knew what to do. She leaned toward Keith and kissed him again, a long, slow kiss that Keith became lost inside. He didn't know what she was thinking and worried for a moment that he was now meant to be the groom. Would he take Don's place? Could it be that simple? Keith wished it was, but that had always been his mistake, thinking love was a straightforward transaction, when really it was as complicated and mysterious as the workings of a living body.

Then Caroline pulled away and gazed at him fondly, patiently, making it clear that her kisses were not what he had thought, but were meant to turn him inside out nonetheless. His heart in all its confusion lay open there before his friends in the hotel room in Reno and he wasn't sure what to make of things anymore.

He then dared to take a glimpse at Don and let out a puff of surprised air. His friend was smiling quite broadly now, his head tipped back, and his eyes bright. Don was reveling in Keith's confusion, just as he always had. This was the old Don, the one Keith had known all along, blessing him with his happiness. What had Keith been waiting for? Don seemed to ask. Why hold back any longer?

Keith felt a tangle of electric currents that ran through him and reached out to the others. He wanted to show how grateful he was to his old friend, and how foolish he had been not to realize there was no time left. But Caroline simply stretched her fingers over Keith's hand as it rested on Don's chest, binding them together in that gentle grip. She relaxed into him, and to Keith's amazement, she shut her eyes. A moment later, Don's eyes closed again, too. The newlyweds rested together that way, perfectly still and quiet.

Keith remained alert and stunned, though exhausted now, too. For a long while, he lay awake with the awareness that he was alive, revived by the touch of Caroline's skin and the pulse of Don's heart beneath his palm. Although their eyes were shut, Keith had the strangest sensation that his friends were keeping watch over him, too, just as he was keeping watch over them, this magical pair. He studied Don's face and tried to burn it into memory. Then, as the hours wore on and the snowstorm tapered off outside, Keith finally let himself rest peacefully.

In the early morning, he awoke with a start to hear Caroline crying softly beside him. Keith listened to the hiss of the oxygen machine and wanted it to be Don's breathing. He moved closer and leaned his ear to his friend's chest, but it already was as hard as a shell, cavernous and hollow with his absence. Keith lifted the sheet over Don's face and took Caroline's hand.

They moved together to the second bed where Keith lay on his back with Caroline curled against his side. She cried and Keith let the tears come, too, ignoring the wetness that pooled on his collarbone. They would call an ambulance when daylight came, because that was what you did, but there was no rush. He and Caroline didn't speak, and after a while, Keith sensed that she might have fallen asleep again, or perhaps she lay awake as he did, watching the gray morning slowly infuse the room's darkness.

In full daylight, Keith pulled back the window curtains to see the sun climbing into a cloudless blue sky. The brightness outside was almost unbearable as drifts of brilliant white snow covered every surface. Keith parted the curtains all the way so the glare would find them with its painful rays. He opened the motel room door and let the crisp, chilly air rush in. Caroline came to stand beside him on the threshold and Keith put his arm around her shoulder. Together they studied the unspoiled parking lot and the world beyond it. They listened for the distant snowplow as it approached from up the road, clearing paths so they might move forward into that day and all the days to come.

Crying in Italian

S ara's new Italian sandals have heels she knows no sane American tourist would attempt on cobblestones. Yesterday the Roman shoe salesman assessed her calves with an unreconstructed male gaze culminating in a subsequent nod of approval—as if her legs had been put on this earth for his pleasure, which she knew was also wrong in every possible way and for which she now pays the price with a sore back and unsteady gait.

Had she even thought about her legs like that in months, perhaps years? The children grab at her skirt and shoulder bag as her husband hurries on ahead in the wake of the tour guide. Sara answers her own question: on a rocky path in the Roman Forum, an American woman jettisons her sensible shoes and doesn't have a clue which way to turn.

"*Gelato*," her son Graham says, for the umpteenth time.

"*Gelato*," little Rachel repeats.

They buzz around her like the bees in the Villa Borghese that very morning. Rachel was stung, something so shocking to her that her eyes welled up with indignation more than pain. Sara longs for such shock, although like the sandals, she suspects that the aftermath would hardly be worth it.

Under the shadow of a cross that rises from the ruins, as if Christianity itself were a monumental afterthought, she saunters toward the tour group, drawn not so much by the sights as by the sweat beading routinely, handsomely, on the guide's brown neck. At the back of the group, her husband Richard appears rapt, his whole being hung on the guide's every stilted English phrase.

"I can't do this anymore," Sara whispers.

Richard wheels around, letting the crowd go ahead to the next sight without him. "What? Why? We have to keep up."

"You go ahead."

He looks perplexed yet sincere, as if seeing one more ancient pile of rubble will answer anything. Sara thinks he wants them to carry on by simply going forward.

"I'll wait in the shade with the kids," she says. "We'll meet you outside the Colosseum."

"Here, take some euros."

"What for?" Sara gestures at the ancient olive trees, the dry landscape, the spiky weeds poking through stones unmoved for all time.

"Get the kids something from the snack carts," Richard suggests and turns to them. "What do you think, guys, you want some *limonata*?" His accent hurts Sara's ears, he's trying so hard. She knows she is being uncharitable, but perhaps, she considers, that's who she is now.

The children huddle, deciding if their longing for *gelato* can be satisfied by *limonata* instead. That's the question, isn't it? she thinks. Can one high, desperate longing be satisfied by something else instead?

Sara's husband gives her coins from his jangling pockets. He is generous, always has been. It makes her wonder how they'll resolve things. Amicably, she suspects.

Graham reaches his sweaty hand into hers for the money. Coins fall to the pebbled ground and Richard tells him to cool it and to pick up the change for his mother.

"All right, you guys," he adds, "I'll see you in forty-five minutes over at the entrance to the Colosseum. Help Mommy find me, all right?"

Then he looks at Sara and presses her purse against her hip, ever mindful of the notorious Roman pickpockets, although their family stands alone on the path. He lowers his voice and leans in closer. "You seem a little out of it today. I'll take the kids later so you can nap. But stay alert now, OK? Don't get lost." His expression is as searching and mystified as when he gazed up at the Sistine Chapel ceiling earlier that day.

Sara nods slowly, noncommittally, the latent teenager in her unwilling to offer more. She knows she's being a brat and wishes he would recognize it, too. Richard turns and scurries up the trail and the children and Sara watch him go. She tries to picture that this is how it will be from then on.

Over the past week, their family has stumbled into dark medieval churches looking for the finger bones and femurs of saints, the preserved bodies of bishops still in their robes, their wax faces surprisingly plump considering there's nothing inside. The bodies are hollow, eviscerated, and yet people kneel before them and close their eyes.

Graham pulls on Sara's purse and jolts her back to the moment. "Euros, Mom. We're dying of thirst."

For an eleven-year-old, he has the presence of someone much older, she thinks, packing all the punch his father lacks. Somehow Sara knows her son will be all right. And little Rachel will be too young to remember. She will try to recall her parents together from snapshots on trips like this one—the picture this morning in front of the fountain in the Villa Borghese. Their separation will mix in her mind with that first bee sting and the Mediterranean heat, all mysterious and conveying a pain that startles, but eventually envelops, like humidity on the skin.

Graham takes the coins and grabs Rachel's hand. They dash off up the path. At least they have each other, Sara thinks.

"Slow down," she shouts after them. "I need to keep you in sight."

"Don't worry, Mom," Graham shouts back over his shoulder.

"Yeah, Mom, don't worry," Rachel copies. Her voice rises and tangles in the olive branches where the sparrows twitter at midday.

As Sara meanders after them, she notices off to the side of the path a flight of ancient stone steps leading up an embankment to nowhere. At the top, a young Italian couple stands close together, their arms around one another. What a romantic sight, she thinks, the woman with sunlight in the folds of her summer dress. Sara pauses and gazes up at them, prepared to smile and sigh, then move on. The young man wears sleek black pants and Sara notices the way his browned forearms and smooth forehead glisten. The girl rises on her toes to reach him and Sara can understand why.

As they kiss, she notices how the young man's hand curves over the young woman's hip. It presses down her thigh and disappears into the fabric between her legs, the small purple flowers embroidered on the white background crimped against his outstretched fingers. Her skirt will be wrinkled, Sara thinks, and quickly feels embarrassed that she is the only one who cares. Any initial thought that this was a tame embrace vanishes as the girl lets out a throaty laugh and squeezes the man's shoulder in a claw-like grip. He does not smile and, what's more important, does not remove his hand from between her legs.

Sara stays frozen on the path, enthralled. She glances down at her new sandals covered now in fine, ancient dust. Something about them on her is as outrageous as the kissing couple, she thinks, and lets out a surprising laugh, too. It's far quieter than the girl's, but every bit as guttural and real. Sara rubs the toe of a sandal against the back of her leg, warm from the sun and firm.

When she looks up again, the couple has moved away from the steps and crossed a ledge overlooking a deep archeological pit. To arrive at their next stopping spot, Sara sees that they've slipped around a low rope barrier and entered an area where tourists aren't allowed. She can't help wondering what they think they're doing there in a forbidden area with groups of tourists drifting by on the paths below.

Without thinking, Sara heads off the central path, too. She hurries up the stairs to keep the couple in sight. Each stone step is high and as she ascends, her skirt catches air and flares outward. With heat billowing around her, her thighs feel damp and shadowed and secret beneath the light fabric. When she reaches the top step, she realizes that she now is exposed, too, her purpose unclear. When she looks across at the couple she is glad to see they haven't noticed her.

They stand, locked in an embrace at the edge of the cliff beside the pit. The man has bent his dark head into the woman's neck and appears to be feasting there. The neck looks startlingly white against his black hair, and then Sara notices the actual lips and open mouth as he kisses the woman's skin. The wetness of his tongue on her cool neck, Sara thinks. That's all she thinks, because it is a thought unto itself: attention must be paid to that tongue and those lips and the press of his body against hers, his hand at the small of her back, pulling her towards him, her dress hiked up, the girl's leg up now, too, and the pretty violets smashed.

Sara looks away and still can't fathom what they think they're doing, what she is doing. They can't make love there on that cliff, can they? she wonders. Or do people do that in Italy, because it is Italy? Perhaps, like her new sandals, allowances are made for such things—sex and passion woven into everyday life. She finished reading Ferrante's *Neapolitan Quartet* on the plane ride over and keeps catching herself searching for tangled, hidden passion everywhere she looks. In Rome, secrets lay as stacked and layered and porous as the crumbled walls of archeological digs.

Early that morning, metal shutters clattered as the shop opened up downstairs. Voices like none Sara had ever heard before echoed off the alley walls, busting wide apart the day. Arguing voices asking only for some milk. If she shed tears, she knows they wouldn't translate: any crying in Italian evaporates, unshed in the scorched air. Swallows swoop past now, disrupting thought and whatever is left of her former self.

When she looks up again, the couple is moving on. The man has the woman's pale hand in his and he's steering her further across the ledge. Sara spots a grove of olive trees in the near distance and imagines he will take her to that quiet spot, where the rocky ground appears to give way to soft grass. He will ease her to it and the girl will pull him down.

Sara can feel the young man's hand, the force of it pressing against her thighs. He pushes her back, hair outstretched like a virgin's on a sacrificial slab. Only nothing about the couple is virginal, and certainly nothing about Sara is, either, which is why she wants to step over the rope barrier, teeter across the precarious ledge, and join them in the partially hidden incline that has been used for this purpose since time immemorial. Only in her own country, in her own stark life, would someone hesitate, Sara thinks, as she hesitates. Yet here she would do it, she tells herself, surely she would.

Then she looks back and realizes she can't see the main path that leads to the *limonata* carts or the plaza where Richard will be meeting them shortly. Sara can't see the kids any longer. She scrambles along the rocky hillside, clomps hastily down the stacked steps, and hurries back onto the trail again. Her greatest fear in this moment is that Richard will have left the tour early and discovered the kids alone by the snack carts. Her absence, she thinks, will prove something undeniable about her. A recklessness and irresponsibility that show she is a bad mother. Richard has recently accused her of being untethered. He doesn't know the half of it.

In the days before their trip, she lost the car keys three times, accidentally shut the cat in the garage overnight, and forgot to pick up Graham from soccer again. She left a flame on under an empty pot and kept the water going in Rachel's bath until a gray cloud appeared on the dining room ceiling. Richard may never know the details, but he grasps the overall effect: she's lost, perhaps dangerously so.

Sara slows on the path and tries to consider the truth. She has been leaving for some time now, so much so as to be already almost gone. It's a wonder she's here at all. But she is a mother and a mother needs to be present. She needs to watch over her kids who, she reminds herself with another jolt, are nowhere in sight. The thought of her imminent and justifiable punishment rises before her: he will get the kids if she doesn't get her shit together.

Sara hurries up the trail and pushes through the turnstile that leads out of the Forum, glancing at the souvenir and snack carts that circle the cobblestones. And look, she thinks, there are her children, bent over their drinks, the long, serpentine straws curving into their mouths. As she approaches, she hears the happy slurping, the pull of the syrupy liquid to their young lips.

Then Sara realizes those aren't the sounds at all: instead of satisfaction, the burbling noise she hears is crying. She dashes forward and crouches down in front of Rachel. Her daughter's face is red from the sun, but her cheeks are dry and her expression seems far too old for her age. Sara turns quickly and sees the last thing she expects: Graham's face streaked with tears. She grabs her son by the wrist, not meaning to frighten him, but he lets out a cry and drops his drink. Yellow liquid spills onto the cobblestones like urine.

"What's wrong?" Sara asks. "Did a bee sting you, too?"

Graham's narrow shoulders heave and he tosses himself against her. Sara rocks back on her heels and lands on her ass on the hard cobblestones.

"Graham," she says, starting to scold him, but something in his shaking body stops her. Sara tries to peel her son off her chest so she can see him better, but he won't let go.

"Rachel," she says over his shoulder. "Tell Mommy what happened."

Her daughter bows her head lower toward her drink and lets out an old lady's worried sigh.

"Did you spend all the money your father gave you? Is that it? You can tell me. I won't be angry with you."

She rubs a hand over Graham's hair and he flinches.

"Children," Sara tries more seriously, "if you won't tell me what's going on, I'll have to ask one of the grownups here." She spreads her arm towards the milling strangers, not one bit sure her meager Italian could do the job.

Her son yanks himself away and he shakes his head hard and scowls.

"Oh, for God's sake, darling, it can't be all that bad," Sara says, her voice harsher than intended. She knows she shouldn't have wandered off, but really, can it be all that terrible?

Graham wipes his cheeks with his forearm and looks at her, pausing for what has to be dramatic effect. "You don't know, Mom," he finally says. "You'll never know."

Sara can't help it, but she laughs. Not a lot, and not loud, but enough. She wants to tell her eleven-year-old that he can't possibly understand the extent to which no one will know, no one will ever understand. The cruelty of her own laughter dawns on Sara a little too slowly and she stops abruptly. The children watch her, worried, perhaps even scared.

She suddenly feels exquisite sympathy for these small people, although in this moment it is hard to grasp that they are hers. Her son's words, spoken so firmly, seem foreign to her. She simply doesn't get their meaning. She wants to believe that they are spoken not to inflict pain, but are the pain itself. But even that motherly understanding, she thinks, is lost in this untranslatable moment.

Sara looks past the children. For an instant, the Colosseum recedes into the distance and the cobblestones that fan out around her rise into a wall that encircles her children. She senses they are disappearing down an ancient stone tunnel. She must reach for them before they are sucked away from her and into a rough-hewn quarry where the innocents are taken. It's a crazy thought, she thinks. The heat is getting to her, dehydration and the pain in her back.

She looks over at the man who runs the *limonata* cart, hoping he can help return her children to her. She will buy more sugary drinks from him to set things right. Gray stubble shades his face and his eyes are hidden under a plaid cap. Sara sizes him up and wonders if he is the culprit who has harmed her son. Yes, he is the dangerous one. But then the old Italian man smiles down at a little girl who stands beside her mother politely waiting for her drink. Sara notices the mother holds her daughter's hand, and she thinks, That should have been me. I should have been that mother, thanking the lemon man.

So if the lemon man didn't do it, Sara wonders, who did? A young Algerian in an NYU t-shirt leans against his souvenir truck, his head bent into his cell phone. Under the shade of an ancient tree, the ubiquitous matrons dressed in black shake their heads at some long-repeated tale. A blond, Northern European family sits wedged together on a bench, eating their sandwiches on dark bread.

Which one of these people stole my son's change from his hand, Sara wonders, or tried to sell him something illicit, or yelled at him needlessly? Which one is a pervert or a pedophile, a nightmare come true? It must have been the lemon man, she thinks again. He is the bad guy. Although now he is whistling as he unloads bright lemons from a wooden box.

She decides she will interrogate him nonetheless in a language he doesn't understand. She will shout at the old man in English and blame him and insist he explain why this country of fine wines and routine epiphanies has not moored her more successfully to her life. Give me back my son, my family, Sara will shout, when really it is herself she wants returned. That's when her husband steps into her line of sight. He looks plain and well-intentioned, familiar and somehow right.

"That was fascinating," he says, nodding over his shoulder at the Colosseum that has righted itself again and appears appropriately colossal.

He leans forward and offers a peck to the air near Sara's cheek. Instinctively, and for no good reason, she leans toward him, too.

She looks down at Graham to try to understand what has happened between them while his father has been gone. Her son stares up at her with an adult expression, one that shows he has things under control now. He surreptitiously wipes away any sign of tears.

"Everything all right?" Richard asks, glancing at each of them. "Is something wrong?"

"No," Graham says firmly. "We're good. Mom bought us lemonade. Mine spilled, but it's no big deal."

Graham offers a manly shrug. He is protecting her, Sara realizes. Something bad has happened and he is covering it up for her sake. Something has come between us, something terrible, Sara thinks. A flicker of understanding passes over her as she wonders if that something is her.

Richard looks to her for an explanation, but Sara is at a loss. She looks to Graham again, and after a long moment, she nods in agreement with him that they are fine. Graham and Sara have made a pact. In one brief moment, her son has become fully-grown and capable of deception, as well as sacrifice and love.

But, Sara reminds herself, I am his mother, not his accomplice. Now is the moment to speak up, to set things straight. The voices of strangers, the wings of birds flapping as they rise to the triumphal arch, the chatter of birds as they settle on the cross casting a shadow on the path, the guides explaining significant moments in history to the interested tourists, the calls of the street vendors: Sara must speak above it all. And yet she stalls. She's still not sure what to say. She stands frozen and feels nothing until Graham steps forward and takes her hand.

"Let's go, Mom," he says. "Time to go."

Sara looks down and wishes she could move forward, take a firm step in her new sandals.

"All right, then," Richard says as he takes Rachel's hand. "We've got just enough time to catch the next bus back to the hotel."

"We're coming," Graham answers for his mother as he starts to pull them up the ancient stones.

"Richard," Sara finally says. "Wait."

Graham looks up at her, his face dark with adult betrayal. He tries again to pull her onward, to march them into the future he assumes is theirs.

Sara turns to her husband, opens her mouth, and begins.

White Dog

A mud-splattered jeep pulled around the circular drive, and William Dunster, his thin frame crumpled in on itself and his mop of white hair flowing, thrust his feet out the open passenger side. The soles of his worn army boots scuffed along the cobblestones as his granddaughter slowed the jeep.

"Hold up now, sugar," he shouted as he slid off the seat and landed on wobbly legs.

Roxanne threw it into park and hurried around from the driver's side to grip his elbow and guide him up the flagstone front walk. Despite a stiff spine, Dunster tipped his head back and gazed up at the mansion before them.

"Looks like I've been on the wrong end of the business all these years," he said and let out a low whistle.

"Not anymore," Roxanne said and squeezed a little too hard. "That's why we're here."

In her tidy skirt with her hair pulled back into a tight ponytail, Dunster hardly recognized his granddaughter. Half a dozen crusty little holes marked each of her earlobes like far-off constellations. He wondered about the tattoos that swirled over her shoulders and were hidden now beneath crisp sleeves. Dunster knew he should be glad she'd finally gotten her act together, but the sight of this polished Roxanne made him unspeakably sad. Why, he wondered, did success have to suck the life out of you?

From somewhere behind the house, two gunshots sounded rapidly, one after the other. Dunster flinched and Roxanne steadied him. "Enemy's closer than we thought," he mumbled.

Roxanne offered a feeble laugh, but Dunster could tell that the shots and the impressive house were making her nervous, too. Together they mounted the marble steps and stopped before the oversized teak door. They studied the chandelier that hung from the ceiling of the two-story portico.

"The castles of the nouveau riche have been the same down through the ages," Dunster said. "Pure plantation house mentality, that's what this is."

Roxanne slapped the bulky sleeve of his army jacket. "That's enough. Not another word on that subject."

"I have no problems with him being a darky," Dunster whispered, "or a gook, or sheikh, or whatever he is. I'm just saying that every culture has its lords and its vassals and this here fellow wants us to know which one he is, and which one he most certainly is not."

Roxanne reached for Dunster's frayed lapels and turned him toward her. "If you so much as hint at this line of thought, I will whisk you out of here so fast you won't know what hit you. You hear me?"

Now there was the tough little cookie he'd helped to raise, Dunster thought with pride. He nodded and swayed and she steadied him. At seventy-four, various ailments had returned, including inner-ear trouble from Korea, the sound of bomber engines still humming in his head. It affected his balance: he couldn't stand straight any longer without teetering like a drunk, which he also was, although only moderately so at the moment.

Roxanne used a manicured fingernail to pick crust from the inner corner of his eye. Ever since his third wife had left him, Dunster knew that his physical appearance had gone south. He'd always been sloppy. If he remembered right, he'd worn his shirttails out at his MoMA opening decades before, but now, he had to concede, he looked borderline homeless. Back when he was young, his thick head of what a woman had once called gloriously flaming hair and his perennially disheveled clothing had entered the consciousness of the art world. They were as ingrained in the minds of the cognoscenti as his abstract paintings of burning crosses, or the white-on-white-on-black landscapes. That he was from mountain people deep in the Ozarks had been part of the mystique back when he was boyish and graceful and as thin as a willow by a rippling creek. He was still thin, even skeletal, and looked a little too much like what he had become: a tired old man who, more often than not, drank too much and forgot to take his meds.

Roxanne rang the bell and a few moments later the door swung open and Rob Singh bowed low before them. He wore a startlingly white linen shirt and a silver pendant on his brown, exposed breastbone.

"William Dunster," he said. "Welcome. Come in, come in."

After Dunster and Roxanne had stepped inside, Rob held up a crystal carafe of amber liquid and announced, "An old friend, I believe." The late afternoon light happened to catch the crystal decanter, sending out surprising rays that danced off the elaborate brass doorknocker. "A rare Glenfiddich I've set aside in your honor, sir."

Dunster's eyes widened and that same whistle sounded from his lips. "Good Lord," he said. "My, my, my."

Rob set the carafe on the hall table and shook their hands. He always loved this moment when he raised the bar on his own performance and showed a potential client what was in store for them. Rob knew he could be overly theatrical, but that was part of how he'd come to own his gallery at such a young age, and besides, what artist didn't hope they deserved such a show? He squeezed Dunster's bony shoulder now as if they'd survived a long campaign together, as if he had been at Dunster's side through a war that had actually taken place before Rob was even born.

"This is what they gave you, isn't it?" he asked the old painter. Dunster looked baffled, but then Rob clarified. "Your first drink out of POW camp, am I right?"

Dunster's eyes widened even more.

"I've been saving it for this day," Rob said and rocked forward onto the balls of his slippered feet.

"But how did you know?" Dunster asked in a small voice.

"I do my homework," Rob said with a single, raised eyebrow. Then he released a warm smile to show it was all done in good fun. "Truly an honor to have you visit our humble abode, William."

Dunster pulled back his shoulders and regained his composure. "Little cabin you got yourself out here in the woods, I see," he said, glancing around.

Rob gestured up at the chandelier above them and chuckled. "Isn't it awful? The worst of the nineties. We bought it for a song from a Wall Street punk desperate for cash. The man once had more money than taste, but in the end, he had neither. We can't wait to knock it down and start over. A real log cabin would be much better, wouldn't it?"

Dunster stopped smiling and a look of confusion spread over his face again. Always good to keep people guessing, Rob thought, though Dunster seemed both figuratively and literally a little off balance. His granddaughter took his arm and Rob said to her, "Thanks so much for driving your grandfather out to see us. Very kind of you to help orchestrate this long-awaited meeting."

As Roxanne offered her own greeting and thanked him for inviting them, Rob turned to see that his wife, Julia, had stepped from the kitchen and was making her way across the dining room and into the marble-tiled hallway. She looked utterly appealing, Rob thought, in her summer skirt with long, tanned legs and perfectly painted toenails in gold sandals. No signs of a growing belly yet. Rob let himself relax. Julia was here. All would turn out well. Dunster would drink the precious, well-chosen scotch. They would talk about his work, which Rob could discuss with true confidence and vision—two of the traits that had formed the basis of his success over recent years. He was at his best and everything, absolutely everything, was going his way.

"Lovely you could join us," Julia said and shook hands with Roxanne. "Hope you didn't have any trouble finding the drive. We're a bit secluded out here."

"Need a compass and a line of bread crumbs to get back," Dunster said then stepped forward and offered Julia an awkward, avuncular hug, which seemed to surprise her, but made Rob smile.

"What a beautiful setting, but don't you get nervous at night?" Roxanne asked. "I mean, it would freak me out to be way out in the woods like this. I'm such a city person."

"The minute we arrive, we forget all our cares and tensions," Rob said. "Isn't that right, honey?"

Julia offered a delicate laugh.

"All right," Rob said. "We *try* to forget them. I tend to work twenty-four seven wherever I am, but it's great for us to get out of the city."

Julia squeezed Rob's arm and he hoped she knew better than to hold him to anything he said in the presence of a new client. She'd been pushing hard for them to move permanently out to the Connecticut countryside. In her pitch, she described how Rob could commute to work or keep a pied-à-terre in the city, while she could raise the baby here, where she imagined things would be more peaceful and nourishing. She had started pressing him about it on the drive up the night before and hadn't stopped since. In their three years of marriage, Rob had come to learn that his wife was every bit as determined and ferocious about getting what she wanted as he was, although she tried not to show it. Still, he had to admit, she looked lovely in her soft teal and beige tones, so perfect with her blue eyes.

"Shall we go in?" She gestured toward the living room. "Rob can show you his art collection and then we'll sit outside on the patio for cocktails. But, first, if you don't mind." Julia pointed down at a lacquered tray on the floor where a half dozen pairs of slippers sat lined up in perfect symmetry, from child-sized to those for a large man.

"Don't tell me you know my shoe size, too," Dunster said.

Rob bobbed a bit. He loved this part. "I make it my business."

Dunster slapped Rob's back. "You are something, son."

"Roxanne," Julia said, "You might want to try the maroon ones. I'm guessing they'll fit."

Roxanne took off her heels and slipped into a pair with embroidered flowers and beads that matched her outfit perfectly. Rob couldn't have done homework on that, too, although he liked to leave people guessing: who knew what he was capable of?

Then Rob and the others looked down at Dunster's boots. Cracked and covered in dried mud, they didn't look like shoes so much as sculptures, something made in a ceramics studio and fired in a deep pit. The laces were black with grime and the tongue hung out of them like an aged body part better kept hidden. Rob thought that a work crew might be needed to pry them off.

"Oh, I see," Julia said, in an uncharacteristically tactless tone.

"Not a problem," Rob offered, glancing at her. "I'll walk William around the house and we'll meet you ladies on the patio. If you don't see the art this time, we'll have other visits."

Dunster let the younger man take his arm and lead him out the front door. He didn't quite catch all of what Rob was saying because of the buzzing in his ears. The two men followed a flagstone path around the side of the house, past manicured shrubs and a feathery Japanese maple at the corner. For some reason, the young gallery owner was asking Dunster which cigar would best accompany the fine scotch, as if Dunster spent his time considering such things. But still, Dunster did his best to sound knowledgeable and wound up carrying on at some length about his preference for Macanudo Maduro over the more popular Partagas Black Label or La Gloria Cubana. Based on the younger man's Cheshire cat smile, Dunster got the impression he had all three in his cigar case, and perhaps even better types that Dunster didn't know existed. By the time they stepped onto the patio, Dunster had digressed into a story about the old days—what had been imbibed back then, and by whom.

"Every night, Joe Riley drank us under the table," he said. "Until he started sneaking off with that uptown lady from his first big opening. She got him into harder stuff. Of course, I didn't know it at the time. There was always a lot I didn't know. I played the country bumpkin, because, well, I was one. People kept me in the dark. I guess they thought it suited me, and perhaps it did."

Dunster shook his head and wondered what on earth had gotten him onto that strange line of thinking. He didn't need to tell this handsome, young fellow all the ways that he had been lost as a young man, or for that matter, as an old man now, too. But somehow Rob Singh encouraged confidences and Dunster couldn't help himself.

"I never did get it straight if Joe's rich girlfriend was the blonde or that dish with the raven hair," he added with a sigh. Then he looked down at Rob and wondered if he could tell him. There seemed to be no limit to what the young gallery owner might know.

But Rob only smiled. He had become accustomed to hearing intimate stories about the great artists of the twentieth century, although sometimes he still had to pinch himself. He, a boy from New Delhi—all right, a well-off boy from New Delhi who had come to boarding school in America—was now a player in the unfolding story of American art. Someday, someone might even tell the story of this very night when what was to become the successful partnership of a revived, aging artist and a young gallery owner had begun.

Rob studied Dunster as he looked out at the grove of trees and the rolling lawn with woods on all sides. The older man squinted and cocked his head. Rob stood beside him and didn't say a thing. He didn't interrupt. He knew that the silences between them were as important as the words. Dunster made a contented sound, a gentle humming, and Rob was pleased that the artist appreciated the beauty out there.

Rob had bought their country home for the view on evenings like this one, when a breeze made the fine tips of the birch and aspen limbs quiver, hinting of rain that would fall later that night. It would blacken the slate path that led past wild azaleas and rhododendrons to the pond at the edge of the woods. Smoke from burning leaves drifted in from the mysterious countryside nearby and the scene stirred in Rob a collective memory, not of his own childhood, but of some quintessential New England past that he felt could just as easily be his.

The trees alone deserved our attention and respect, he thought. He loved the way the ancient moss softened the roots of the maples that loomed high over the shale outcroppings. As Rob studied the landscape, he decided that the crown canopy overhead, with its shocking orange patches and blood red ones, was outrageous, and yet also impeccably classy—like the gaudy pink and green outfits worn by the old timers out on Nantucket. Rob's property was as refined as any he could imagine. A setting, he had come to understand, that tied him—tied them all—to something deeply American and right. He and Dunster took it in slowly, patiently, the way he might sip a truly fine wine.

That was when the white dog appeared on the lawn for the second time that day. It stood now far to one side in the shadows by the woods. The dog circled, then stopped and stared at them through the trees. Rob stepped forward and clapped his hands. He stomped his feet and tried to shoo it off. But the creature only took a few steps back and continued to look at them.

The women arrived, full of conversation as the screen door scraped open and they stepped out onto the patio. Rob promised Dunster his scotch, offered wine to Roxanne, sparkling water for Julia, and slipped inside to prepare the drinks.

Julia held a tray of various finger foods and Dunster thanked her and took a sizable handful. Roxanne inched her chair closer to his and he could sense her starting to hover. All his life, women had fussed over him, as if his very being were a problem they had been assigned to fix. He had retreated into his studio to escape their ministrations, so he supposed now he owed them some thanks. He was aware that he might have given up as a painter long ago if they'd simply left him alone.

Roxanne tapped his wrist to get him to stop wolfing down the food, or perhaps she was going after it for herself. Dunster popped several more of the crackers with some sort of cheesy spread into his mouth and she quickly handed him a cocktail napkin. He had no use for such things—for most things, actually—so he crumpled it in his large hand and stuffed it into one of the many pockets of his flak jacket.

"Take your time," his granddaughter whispered. "This isn't your last meal." Then to Rob she said, "Vegetarians are supposed to care about what they eat. Not Dunster. He'll eat anything, so long as it doesn't have a face."

Dunster didn't mind what she said. She was flesh and blood and, like Dunster himself, had been through hell and back, so she was all right by him. He chewed and settled deeper into his seat and let the women carry on about second homes and babies while he looked out at the lawn and the trees. He considered the quality of light and the angles of the trunks and the way the lawn looked flat, like a poorly painted surface. The world sometimes played tricks on us, he thought, by imitating itself, and often quite badly. There was something too familiar about this scene, he thought. Quintessentially American and yet fake as a wooden nickel, which, he had to admit, was also truly American. That the gallery owner had fallen for such a stereotype didn't surprise Dunster, although it did sadden him. He had hoped the fellow might have had a deeper sensibility than this stage set suggested.

Absorbed as Dunster was in these thoughts, it took Roxanne placing the glass of scotch into his hand for him to snap to. He smiled up at Rob, who bowed again. They raised their glasses in a quick salute and drank. The scotch tasted as it had that day in the Korean jungle when

Dunster had held the bottle in a trembling hand. It would always taste the same, he thought, which came as a relief. He squinted at the younger man, trying to remember something, and Rob mistook his expression and smiled back.

The boys had always bowed like that when they did things for you, Dunster recalled, like clearing your plate from the table or opening the door for you or pouring your drink. A water boy in a Seoul hotel had accidentally drenched Dunster's lap and was pulled aside, hit with a bamboo cane on his legs, and fired right there in sight of the foreigners. The fools in charge had been trying to impress the Americans, but the moment had only depressed Dunster, recalling the savagery of the POW camp. He drank himself blind that night, but the following morning he had gone to the front desk and berated the hotel manager, insisting they bring back the water boy. The manager had apologized, but said it would be impossible to rehire him. There are far too many boys for us to worry about just one, the man had said. He had already hired another.

Dunster tried to remember more about the incident, but all he could recall with any clarity was the sound of the stick slicing the air as it slapped against the thin calves, and the boy's whimper, which carried across the years along with that phrase: there are far too many to care about just one.

Dunster watched as the white dog moved toward them, weaving slowly through the stand of trees into the nearer distance. Its head was bowed and its thin, white shoulders protruded. The animal stood in shadow, with a dusky mist starting to settle around it. The thing looked more miserable than menacing.

"That's one pitiful soul," he said. "It hurts the eyes just to look at it."

Rob stamped his foot again and clapped, but the dog didn't seem to notice. It did hurt to see it there, he thought, spoiling what should be a perfect evening.

"It seems to like us," Julia said.

"Poor old, mangy thing," Roxanne added.

Dunster mumbled into his glass, "Resembles the dogs we used to eat in Korea."

"Grandpa!" Roxanne said and slapped his arm. "No one wants to hear about that."

"It's all right," Julia said, in a soothing voice. "You can tell us."

Dunster looked at Rob Singh's wife for the first time and saw that she was exceptionally pretty, but perhaps more than that. There was a look of yearning and sadness in her eyes—that was the only way to describe it. If Dunster were to paint her, he thought, he'd keep her perched on the edge of her cast iron seat, clearly uncomfortable as she leaned forward, solicitous and quietly pained.

"Of course, they eat them there," Rob said, perhaps a little too sharply. He thought that by now his wife should know such things were common in Third World countries. The one time she had visited Delhi, he had tried to make that clear to her, but she had been raised in a house not unlike this one, though of an earlier vintage, and had never been exposed to true hardship. Whereas Dunster and he most certainly had seen it and somehow felt its effects—another crucial thing they had in common, Rob thought, in addition to understanding art.

"The guards considered them a delicacy," Dunster continued. "We were grateful when they gave us a few bites. Sickens me now to think of it."

"How awful," Julia mumbled.

His wife's tender voice irritated Rob. Dunster didn't need coddling. The older man needed someone who grasped what he had been through—the lows, not just the highs—and knew enough not to dwell on it, but instead, was determined to push him forward into the future and out of the muck of the past.

"Come on now, it wasn't your fault. You were starving," Rob said to clear up the matter. "It's best to forget about such things."

Dunster nodded and drank, but then, after a long moment, he added, "You don't know how low you'll go, until you do."

Rob tapped the rim of his scotch glass against his teeth and worried that the conversation had become too somber too fast. When he looked over, though, and noticed Dunster eyeing him, Rob realized that the older man had been speaking just to him and what he had said was important and true. For although Rob couldn't say how he knew it was true, he did. His life, truth be told, had been full of good fortune, but still, he knew he would do something desperate if that ever changed. He was forever at the ready for just such a turn, because such things did happen, even to the most prepared of people. He, like Dunster, knew what was required of him. You don't know what you'll do, until you do it. They both understood that.

"I hear they still eat them in the restaurants over there," Dunster said, a more jovial tone returning. "People know what to ask for. It's not printed on the menu."

The two men chuckled and the women offered sad little exhalations of air. Then they all looked out at the dog. The creature seemed to hang its head even lower, taunting them with its ugliness. Rob wanted to go to the barn and bring out the hunting rifle again. Earlier, right before his guests had arrived, he had shot a few rounds up into the trees to scare the creature away. It had worked for a little while, but now the beast had slunk back into sight. Rob thought he might have to try that again. But now he didn't want to leave Dunster's side, didn't want to disrupt the momentum of the evening and their courtship dance.

Rob pulled his metal chair closer to Dunster's and dove right in. He asked about the painter's recent work. He wanted to know everything: the precise use of each medium, the way Dunster conceived his compositions, and the intention behind each choice along the way. He had to understand what currents had led Dunster from his earlier pieces to this latest body of work. This was Rob's favorite part of what he did. He knew he had a reputation for being a savvy businessman. Some even said that it didn't matter what he sold, he'd always make a killing. But the truth was, it mattered very much to him what he promoted.

He cared about the art, and even about the artists, at least some of them. He wasn't sure why, but it was like the landscape on his property: he felt it was his job to help preserve and protect a dying breed, or a breed that was colossally ill-suited to the realities of the twenty-first century. He excelled at speaking the language of the artist, and then he took it upon himself to translate what he had learned into the language of the wealthy patrons who wanted to be initiated into the art world, but didn't know how. For his customers, he was a guide, a priest, even a soothsayer. But first and foremost, he always presented himself as a student, an apprentice, or even a supplicant before the artists he chose to represent.

So Rob continued with his questions and Dunster raised a bushy eyebrow and began to rattle off his replies. Right off the bat, it was obvious to him that the young gallery owner was serious about his job. He seemed intent on getting the full story behind each work, which impressed the old man. Most of the time these days, people didn't give a shit about process. They only wanted the end product, which truthfully had never mattered all that much to him. He was a painter. He liked to paint. The very act of painting gave him solace in life like nothing else he had ever encountered, even sex, though he'd never mentioned that to a soul.

He knew rumors used to fly about his early friendships with his fellow artists, and while the particulars were wrong, it was a fact that he had never felt closer to any other human beings than that particular group of guys. They mattered more to him than his three wives, even the one he had truly loved, or his daughter, or granddaughter. That was just the way it was. And all because of process: loving the process, or the process of loving. Dunster wasn't sure which, but he was getting off track, and needed to concentrate because the kid was fired up with more questions, smart ones, challenging ones.

Dunster hadn't had a conversation like this since the old days when he, Riley, Truscott, Freed, and the others used to get together every evening to get drunk and talk about the day's headway. They didn't discuss ideas so much as what worked. Sharing what each had figured out that very day. And if there were a sale going on of paint somewhere nearby, they'd share that, too, or where to find scrap lumber, or the location of a demolished building to scavenge. They were tradesmen. And now there was a brass plaque about them on the New York condo where the Cedar Tavern used to be, and a PBS documentary about the early days. Dunster shook his head and marveled at the strange passage of time—how a life could rise and fall in what felt like a matter of hours.

Rob Singh's wife came around with the tray of hors d'oeuvres again and Roxanne smiled a little too obviously when Dunster took only one. He drank slowly now, but with purpose. This young Rob fellow was all right and he appeared poised to see that Dunster had another chapter, albeit a final one, in his life as an artist.

After Rob apologized for grilling Dunster with questions, and Dunster had said that he was flattered, a silence took over again. Dunster felt good as he waved his drink at the darkening trees and the dusky lawn and asked, "So, tell me, how in God's name did you wind up here?"

Dunster watched the younger man look out at the fussed-with, perfect landscape that he clearly adored. Then it was Rob's turn to talk, to explain how he had made his way up the ladder to this great height. It had started when Joe Riley—Dunster's Joe Riley—was a visiting art teacher at Rob's boarding school. Dunster vaguely recalled Riley taking off for some place outside the realm of anyone's interest. As it turned out, his friend had been cagey and ambitious. The gig at the boarding school had helped him rise to a better gallery, and soon Riley became known to the patrons themselves, and the party invitations had started rolling in. He had tried to get Dunster to tag along, but Dunster had demurred. He stayed downtown in his loft, painting till dawn and eating meals out of takeout boxes. Dunster could see now that right around the time Rob Singh was starting to get to know Riley, Dunster was starting to lose him. That didn't seem like a coincidence, but Dunster wasn't sure what it meant.

In the end, Riley was the first to go, the drugs shortening the life of things for him considerably. Such a goddamn shame, Dunster thought. What he wouldn't give to be sitting there right now with his old friend on that patio, looking out at this ridiculous view. The young Riley would get the joke of the house and the yard and the sincere gallery owner who peppered the description of his life with the first names of the rich and famous.

But Dunster needed to pay attention and catch up with the stream of Rob's words. Apparently, back at the prep school, Riley had taken a handful of students into the city and toured them around the galleries on 57th Street. Rob had watched the way Riley was treated by those elegant people, how he was part of a secret society, and how knowing the art mattered, but the real reward was in knowing the people, such smart and intriguing people. Rob had wanted that for himself ever since.

The young Indian boy wasn't content to pour the water, but instead wanted to take a seat at the table with the other Americans: that seemed right, Dunster thought, good for him. That's how it should be. Rob continued to explain that as a young man, he had joined that same world and while the people had mostly intimidated him, he remembered how glamorous it had been. So he kept striving and learning and making his way.

Dunster understood the impulse, but unlike Rob, he had realized pretty early on that it wasn't the people who sustained you. It was the work. The work—the ongoing lover's quarrel with the work—was what mattered. Riley had lost track of that and it didn't take long for it to do him in. But way back before Riley had been sacrificed to the great gods of commerce and the vipers of the art world, Dunster, like Rob, had been tempted by the magical, unending party that he, too, had stumbled on when he first arrived in New York.

"I watched and I learned," Rob was saying as he described his early position at a blue-chip gallery. "I made some smart bets along the way, chose my artists carefully, did my homework, and was daring at just the right moments. There are times when you must step up to the plate and do what needs to be done."

"And also luck," his wife added, leaning forward in her seat so her head was no longer in shadow. "We've been awfully lucky."

The plaintive expression had appeared again on her pretty face, Dunster noticed, and he wished he could reach over with a paint rag and wipe it off. That's what she needed, someone to soothe her furrowed brow. Such a beautiful young woman, he thought, should not look so troubled. Dunster was glad when Rob reached over and took his wife's hand.

But then the gallery owner said, "No, that's not it, honey. It has nothing to do with luck. Am I right, Dunster? It's the work: that's what it's all about. The work."

Rob's wife slipped her hand free from her husband's and Dunster thought he could feel the emptiness it left behind. His wives would have done the same thing. Rob was behaving like the kind of man that Dunster had once been. Sure of himself to the point of cockiness about the most insignificant of matters, all the wrong things. Anything to win an argument. How foolish men were not to notice the look on a woman's face. Couldn't they see it? Dunster wondered now. He supposed they could not, because he hadn't, repeatedly.

Dunster simply smiled at his host now and hoped he wasn't really supposed to reply. The scotch was getting to him in a good way and he'd done enough speechifying already. He must have spouted his usual one about the work, because young Rob Singh was repeating it back to him. Dunster nodded along, though when Rob talked about the crucial importance of the work it somehow felt tainted. Dunster wasn't sure why, but he sensed that Rob didn't know what he was talking about. How could running a gallery be anything like working on a painting? It irked Dunster and he took another long sip.

Rob felt satisfied that the artist agreed with him, although when he looked at his wife he could see that she still wasn't convinced. But of course Dunster would understand, Rob thought, because William Dunster had come from out of nowhere, too, and he had fallen for the same great, fast game. He had succeeded at it, too, at least to a certain extent. Rob looked at the grizzled face of the older man and thought he could see in it the artist's younger self, the one pictured in the group photos of the thin, confident men from that earlier time. Dunster was always off to one side, the youngest, an outsider even among those who fancied themselves outsiders. Rob knew what it had taken for Dunster to persist and it wasn't luck.

"The work can kill a man if he isn't careful," Dunster finally said.

"Exactly," Rob said.

"Kill a man, even if he is."

Rob wasn't as sure about that idea.

"You wind up like that dog out there," Dunster said, lifting his glass toward the yard. "Look at it: just asking to be killed and eaten. If he happened to be in the wrong place, that'd be the end of him. He has no idea how lucky he is to be a goddamn American dog."

Rob looked out again at the misty and shadowed grove of trees. The dog had come closer, its head still drooping and its ribs rising and falling with each breath. He knew what Dunster was getting at, but the animal didn't look American to him, at least not the kind of America Rob wanted to think about. It looked hungry. Worse than hungry. Maybe even starving and clearly from a different, terrible place altogether.

Rob noticed that Dunster had sunk lower in his seat, hunkered down, the alcohol getting to him. They needed to feed him a proper dinner, get him upbeat again. All this talk of the old days was taking its toll on the painter, whose career, let's face it, had slowed considerably. Rob would bring the conversation around, show the bright future ahead.

But then he turned and looked out again at the yard.
They all looked out. Everything was dull grayness now,
except for the dog's shabby white coat, which seemed to
grow brighter as all around it became shrouded by an
oncoming mist and nightfall. The creature swayed beside
the nearest tree. Rob wanted them to carry on about the
art and the way their paths were converging for a reason.
But they had briefly lost their way as they sat and let the
dog stare them down.

Julia finally broke the silence, speaking more to
Dunster's granddaughter than to the men. "I put some
cat food out for it earlier today," she said. "The minute I
stepped away, it snuck over and wolfed it all down. So I
brought out another can and the same thing happened,
the poor thing was starving."

"That's so sweet of you," Roxanne said. "I would've
done the same thing."

"Wait," Rob said and turned to his wife. "You fed it?"

She took a quick sip of sparkling water.

"We're trying to get rid of it, honey," Rob said. "We
can't have an animal around that looks like that."

Dunster reached for the crystal carafe of scotch and
poured himself another two fingers.

"Of course I fed it," Julia said. "Anyone would do that,
especially out in the countryside. People are decent here."

Rob could feel the vein in his neck pulsing. He couldn't
believe his wife was choosing this moment to air their
argument about where to live once the baby came. She'd
be bored within a week and there was no way he could
exist away from the gallery. She was making no sense.
"Julia," he said sharply. "That has nothing to do with this."

She sat straighter and said, "No harm in being nice is
all I'm saying."

Rob set down his glass so firmly the table rocked on
the flagstone patio. He spoke with great control. "That

dog is more than an eyesore. It's a menace. It might have rabies. I'm talking about protecting my family."

Julia crossed her tan ankles and tried to smile. "Rabies, I don't think so. I bet it was abandoned or ran away from an abusive home or something." She looked at Roxanne for corroboration. "Who knows why it would look like that? But it's not the animal's fault."

Rob exhaled.

Roxanne pulled a strand of hair from her bun and twisted it around a finger. She reached for the bottle of wine on the table and poured herself another glass. Then she tapped Julia's knee and said, "Stray cats find me all the time. And I mean all the time. I've kept about as many as I've taken to the shelter over the years. I can't seem to turn them away."

Rob felt that with each passing moment, he was losing Dunster. The older man had slumped more and appeared to be in a staring contest with the white dog on the lawn. Rob worried that the old painter was becoming drunk on the animal's pathetic aura. Rob could not allow the mangy beast to steal his artist. Finally, he could restrain himself no longer.

He pointed at the dog and said to Dunster, "I find it disturbing to look out there and see that miserable thing defiling a perfect vista."

Dunster squeezed his eyes as if he were trying to see it the way Rob described. He finally offered a slow, steady nod of his great, white head.

"See, William knows what I'm talking about," Rob said to the women. "This is a traditional American landscape, am I right, Dunster?"

"It is."

"And because of that, we want it to look a certain way, don't we? We want it to look the right way." Rob knew that his voice was growing louder and more insistent, but he needed to make a point. "This setting, this canvas, if you will, is meant to be. It *has* to be. There's perfection in it." This was the argument he had to make, the aesthetic purpose that tied them together—he and Dunster. Dunster would understand that this was about art.

Rob was flushed now and although he gritted his teeth, he found pleasure in the growing understanding between himself and the older man. "An interruption, a mistake or weakness trespasses on a perfect picture." Rob stood and waved his scotch glass toward the dog. "All because of this."

"This," Dunster echoed.

"You see, Dunster gets it." Rob hovered for a moment over his wife. He reached for the carafe, refilled his glass and added a hefty splash to Dunster's. "This artist, this great man, understands."

Rob didn't mind Dunster guzzling his fine scotch. He didn't mind him gazing blankly out at his land. They were in agreement on so much: Dunster's art, the paths of their lives coming together, and this common enemy on the lawn. Dunster hadn't gotten to where he was by being faint-hearted, and neither had Rob. Nothing, absolutely nothing, had to do with luck.

"Tell me," Rob asked Dunster, "would you have fed that creature out there?"

Julia started to stand. "Rob," she said.

He pressed a hand on her shoulder and eased her back down into her chair. "I'm sorry, honey, you have a big heart, but you also have certain sentimental notions. We have to be tough in this world. We have to understand what's out there just waiting to ruin us."

Julia's voice quivered but her words were distinct. "I'm not willing to be cruel, if that's what you mean."

Dunster looked from the dog to Julia and appeared to flinch at her words.

"This is between Dunster and me. I'm asking him, not you." Rob turned to the older man. "Would you have gone out there and coddled it?"

Dunster's brow was now as furrowed as Julia's, but after another long sip, Rob thought he saw him shake his head.

"No," Rob said. "I didn't think so, because Dunster and I know what needs to be done."

He set down his glass and marched off into the darkness of the driveway, heading toward the barn. Julia drifted so she stood with her hands on the back of the iron porch chair and watched her husband disappear into the night. Across her thin shoulders, she draped a white cardigan sweater, the old-fashioned type that Dunster's mother had worn. He thought he could still remember the softness of the lightweight summer wool. And something about the way it glowed in the evening darkness felt familiar, too. Her face was in shadow and Dunster wished he could see her eyes, although he suspected he knew how they looked. She sat again, her knees practically touching Dunster's granddaughter as they conferred.

"Man, that dog's really getting to your husband," Roxanne said to Julia. "Nothing like a desperate loser to mess you up. The cats were one thing, but you should have seen some of the guys I used to bring home, right, Grandpa?"

Dunster offered a chuckle and she gave him that quirky, apologetic smile of hers, the same one she'd had all her life. Roxanne was all right, he thought. She, of all of them, was all right. She appeared to have made peace with her past and was moving on. Roxanne accepted that it would cast its shadow over her always, which was correct. You can't run away from it, Dunster understood, the way this young Indian fellow seemed to think you could, remaking yourself entirely for each person you met. That white dog out there knew the score: you were what you were.

Dunster decided in that moment he might just let things slip away. He wasn't sure what he meant by that, but it made him feel happier than he had all evening to consider the possibility: maybe he wouldn't let the powerful Rob Singh remake him in his own image. He would remain Dunster, the unreconstructed old-school wretch who made everyone around him uncomfortable because he was who he was. He'd botched up a good portion of his life, but not all of his paintings. Some of his paintings were quite fine, and he didn't need any young buck to tell him so.

Dunster hummed a few notes, not of any recognizable song, more a drone of repeated sound, joining the clatter of the birds as they came home to roost for the night high up in the treetops. He shook his head gently from side to side and his white hair fell over his forehead. He focused his eyes far off and considered the vanishing point if this had been a painting. But only a fool would paint this scene, he thought again, which, sadly, the young gallery owner was too blind and hoodwinked by America to grasp, because he owned this land and believed in what he thought it stood for. Such rubbish, Dunster thought.

Then Rob returned from out of the dark and stepped from the shadows with a rifle in his hand. He stopped in a shaft of light that cascaded through the sliding screen door. His shirt had come open and on his chest hung the silver pendant. His eyes were shadowed and dark and his face looked tough and unyielding, as if he had traveled a great distance. Now that would make a painting, Dunster thought, one that could transform, and not just translate, what was there before their eyes.

He kept humming and shaking his head from side to side. Roxanne patted his arm and he knew she meant well by it. He was starting to embarrass himself. Dunster sensed it, but an internal rhythm had him now and wouldn't let go.

"Here," Rob said, holding out the rifle and pointing the muzzle up at the sky. "Would you like to do the honors? Two shots into the air did the trick the last time."

Julia stepped forward. "Dunster doesn't want to fire a gun, do you, Dunster? That's not who you are."

Dunster bowed his head and said, "Very kind of you, my dear. You are quite lovely."

When he looked up, he saw that her face was still pained. The poor, young woman, he thought. He stood slowly and this time when Roxanne tried to take his arm, he snapped it away. It was true, he didn't want to fire a gun. Dunster had never wanted to fire a gun, but it had fallen to him before, and it would fall to him again. Rob was right that the war had taught Dunster that. As had the art world. But, really, it was the painting itself that made you tough, if you stuck with it. It hardened you and made you stand on your own two damn feet. Dunster had never felt more ready to stand that way than now. He planted himself and reached out with a trembling hand.

Rob smiled, his white teeth shining. "All yours, my friend."

Dunster gathered the heavy rifle into his hands and braced himself. He hadn't held a rifle in fifty years, but he remembered what to do. Rob was right. Sometimes you just knew what had to be done.

Rob went on, saying, "Two shots into the branches will scare the thing off while we eat dinner."

Dunster wasn't listening. The sound in his ears was as loud as it had ever been. Perhaps louder. He squeezed the trigger and the gun kicked. He staggered and landed hard in his chair and nearly toppled backwards. The women shrieked and looked out at the lawn.

"How could you?" Julia shouted at Rob.

Then she and Roxanne ran out toward the trees. When they reached the lifeless animal they stopped their cries and fell to their knees beside it. Dunster sat sprawled and Rob crouched beside him.

"Are you all right?" he asked. "I should have told you it has a terrible kick."

Dunster hummed softly.

"You didn't mean to do that, did you? You were aiming higher, right?"

Dunster neither shook his head nor nodded as they both stared out at the women kneeling beside the body of the dog.

"No one has to know about this," Rob began, when he finally spoke, his voice hard and controlled. "You made a mistake, that's all. We don't have to mention it ever again. Give it a few weeks, a month. We'll have lunch in the city. You can come by the gallery sometime."

Rob waited for Dunster to respond, but he didn't. He stared out past Rob and into the dark. Rob stood, and as he watched his wife bend over the dead animal, he knew that what he had suspected for some time was true: it was over between them. He couldn't do what he needed to do while being held back and burdened by her. Rob also knew that if he didn't return Dunster's call for days, then weeks, the old man would crawl away into the nondescript woodwork of the art scene. Rob felt relieved to have been spared the embarrassment of working with such an unstable man. He just hoped Dunster would let it go gracefully and not make a scene.

But Dunster wasn't thinking about Rob at all. Instead, the humming had subsided in his head as a hollow sensation took hold. The mist that had curled across the grass all evening now reached his boots and began to envelop him. The breeze had picked up and Dunster listened to the rustling in the dark canopy overhead. Dampness descended with the night and the birds had grown quiet. Rain wouldn't be long now.

He struggled to understand why he'd pulled the trigger. Rob Singh had wanted to preserve his impeccable vista, but didn't he know that perfection smelled like death? With that one shot, Dunster had upped the ante and shown Rob that he was wrong not to make his peace with the smudge on the horizon, the mistake on the canvas. The only way to live was to absorb the mess and the blight and the decay, embrace every imperfection into both life and art. Rob couldn't see it, but Dunster could, and that's what had saved him.

Still, the consequences would need to be reckoned with, as always. With a heavy exhalation, Dunster let go of the idea of Rob Singh and his world. His high-end gallery would go on promoting the paintings of other men. Dunster would return to his work, like a man returning to a kind and steady wife. He didn't deserve her, he knew that, and he meant to do better by her next time, but for now, Dunster would simply return, his tail between his legs.

He looked across at the shadows of the kneeling, sorrowful women and thought that maybe now Rob's wife could go free. Her white cardigan glowed above the dark lawn like a bright spot of paint at the tip of his brush.

An Awesome Gap

Around the corner, the lot opened up and the asphalt smoothed out. The rough patches disappeared and Patrick glided along, gaining speed as he headed for a concrete barrier. A half dozen of them sat angled in different directions, each with its own character and challenge. Patrick loved the soft roar of his wheels, the clack and rattle and bang of the other boards, each skater doing his thing. A bunch of the guys were over checking out a gap beside a dumpster on the other side of the parking lot. Patrick wanted to check it out, too, but no way with his dad still nearby.

He couldn't believe he'd let his dad drive him. He felt his heart speed up and he hated to think of his father waiting for him in his car, as if this was some lame soccer practice. Patrick first said no to the ride, even though buses didn't run to this part of town on Sundays. He'd have gotten here somehow, maybe hitched a ride. He would've figured something out. But then his dad turned it into a family outing and Teddy had to tag along.

"I'm happy to drive you boys to the skate park," his dad had said as they climbed into his new car.

"It's not a skate park, Dad. It's just a spot."

"All right then, skate spot."

"Don't call it that, either. It sounds weird when you say it."

"OK, I'll call it that place you like to go."

"Just don't call it anything."

His father offered a slight smile in the rearview mirror and Teddy let out a giggle. Patrick had pressed his forehead to the car window and seriously considered climbing out at every red light. A few blocks before they reached the spot by the river, he begged to get dropped off, but his dad said the neighborhood was too rough. As soon as he put the car in park, though, Patrick was out of there. He bolted with his board under his arm and hoped no one had seen him arrive.

He shook his head hard now to get focused again. He went up one of the ramps, took it slow to start out, ollied off and landed it. A few more times, same thing, but then Teddy showed up beside him and said, way too loud, "That was awesome, dude!"

Patrick wanted to ditch his little brother so bad. Skate off to the other side and act like he'd never met him before.

"Should we, like, go over there?" Teddy asked, pointing across to the higher concrete barricades where a few of the older guys were skating.

"Don't point, man," Patrick said.

Then he looked down at Teddy and saw him shrink to an even smaller size, if that was possible. Being Teddy had to be painful.

"Let's just skate," Patrick said. "That's what we came here for, dude. You can do it." He squeezed his little brother's thin shoulder. "That three-stair over there is good. You can do that one."

Patrick offered a thumbs up before taking off again. He didn't want to be mean, but he had to get into his own head. Too many fucking distractions, like Teddy and his father nearby. Patrick did a pop shuvit off a crumbling curb and tried to get his legs working. He started toward a gap, got psyched to do a kickflip, and landed pretty decent. Two more times, each one better, so maybe this day wasn't going to suck after all.

He stopped and looked around and noticed two guys standing above a drop, checking it out. One of them nodded. Patrick nodded back. He liked that. Each skater doing his own thing. He headed off again toward a curve of concrete spray-painted with the words *Skate and Destroy*. He took the ramp and did a 180 with decent air. It was better the next time and the time after that and the time after that. On the fifth time, Patrick landed it sketchy, so he stopped and shook out his legs.

The breeze off the river was cold, but it felt good on his sweat. He didn't pause for long, but went after another ramp and did a backside 180 again and again, each time landing it different. As the sun started to slip behind the boarded-up warehouse, he caught his breath. He spat on the ground and looked down at the brown river water, churned up and probably polluted as hell, but he liked it. He liked his town, now that he knew about places like this. Real places where real shit happened. Real people, too, not like in the suburbs where he lived. Not like his parents, who were stuck there twenty-four seven and boring as shit.

Patrick's dad had recently started trying to look hip and cool, which was worse than looking old. Patrick pictured his father pounding away on his laptop propped against the leather steering wheel. His mom said he needed to keep up with the younger guys at the office. They wanted to eat his lunch, whatever that meant. Patrick thought his dad needed to mellow out. Who gives a shit? He'd never be a slave to work like that, always worrying about the future and not doing what he wanted to do right now. Patrick didn't think he wanted to go to college, though that was a long way off. Most of the pros never went. Teddy could go someday, but not him.

No one in his family got it that you had to live in the moment and do what you loved to do. His dad's old darkroom in the basement was filled with Christmas decorations now and he worked all the time to pay for stupid stuff like his new car and pointy shoes. None of those things mattered. It didn't matter what other people thought, Patrick told himself. You just needed to kill it, just fucking kill it, because that's what you did. That's what he'd tell his dad if he ever asked. Then he finally landed one.

About a dozen guys showed up just then from around the corner, skating the ramps, doing 360 flips and hardflips off the ends. These guys were serious and sponsored by the skate shop downtown. Patrick knew them all—not exactly knew them, but knew who they were. There was Jamie Lawrence, one of the best skaters in town, and Billy Wilson, whose photo had made it into *Thrasher*, and Rob Knox, a skateboard legend in his day. These guys didn't know Patrick, though maybe they'd seen him around.

Patrick hadn't told anyone, but he wanted more than anything to skate for the shop team. He wanted to work there, too. And hang out there. Hell, he'd even sleep there. He went all the time, but not so often as to be a pain in the ass like the little boys who still had their moms take them in. He couldn't imagine standing at the counter with his mother asking stupid questions, which she would, even when she promised not to.

Patrick always went in alone and a few of the guys who worked there had started to recognize him. He saved up for new trucks or bearings. On the way over today, he'd kept the extra buck and change from the frosties his father had bought him and Teddy. He'd put it towards a new deck. His dad hadn't even noticed, that's how out of it he was, his mind always on work.

Shit, his dad, Patrick thought. He whipped out his cell phone and looked at the time. Just over an hour. And where the hell was Teddy? He spotted his little brother crouched near where the pros had come in. He must have been sitting there when they swarmed around him, probably scaring the piss out of him. But they wouldn't have noticed Teddy. Who knew why nobody ever noticed Teddy, but they didn't. Patrick headed toward him, dialed his dad, and wished he'd brought some water. He was thirsty as shit.

"Hey, Dad," Patrick said when his father answered his cell phone.

"Patrick? I can't hear you."

Patrick pulled up in front of Teddy and rolled his eyes at his phone. Teddy giggled. "So, hey, can we, like, keep skating?" Patrick asked.

"Son?"

"Dad?"

The cell phone cut off.

"Dumb-ass phone," Patrick said and tucked it into his pocket. "What's happening?" he asked Teddy and offered a fist.

Teddy butted it happily. "This place is amazing. I did that three-stair."

"Nice, bro," Patrick said, letting his words roll out long so Teddy could soak it in. "I knew you could do it."

The pro skaters moved past them and were taking turns being filmed by a dude who skated along next to them as they did their tricks. The camera hung loosely from his hand like a wilted flower and he was drinking a beer, so maybe not a serious shoot. They were just screwing around.

Patrick didn't want to show off or anything, but seeing those guys doing cool stuff made him want to go for something bigger. He took off for one of the ramps and killed it. Then he headed toward the big gap that the skate shop guys had been doing earlier. He hoped they weren't looking his way, or maybe he hoped they were, but he had to just focus as he booked straight up the side. He had an easy approach and was going to get some real air. He knew he could do it. Patrick popped off the ground, spun his board, and tried to get his legs high enough and long enough to land it clean.

When it worked, he felt suspended for a crazy long time. His mind went clear and his body did what it needed to do. But this time, the moment of flying went too fast. He recognized this feeling, too, and hated it. Gravity fucking sucked. His body started to fall before he'd gotten high enough to make his move. His feet flailed as they searched for the board. Patrick came down and the rough surface bit into his hip and hands and shoulder. Although he tried to roll away from the fall, his face skidded on the asphalt and his cheek burned and he bit his bottom lip hard.

"Shit," he moaned and curled on his side, legs pulled up to his chest.

Teddy ran over and bent down. "You all right, Pat?"

Looking up at Teddy from the ground actually made him look big. Patrick wanted to laugh, but he had to swallow hard to keep from crying. His brother's face looked seriously worried. After a minute, Patrick made himself sit up and everything went fuzzy, but got normal again pretty soon. Probably not a concussion, but a shiver rose up his body and he wondered if maybe he was more messed up than he thought.

Teddy reached out and Patrick let him pull him up by his decent hand. He leaned against his brother and started to pick bits of gravel and blood from his cheek and his palm. It stung like hell to pull them out. Patrick shook out his limbs and decided that nothing was broken. His T-shirt was torn at the shoulder, but that didn't matter. He looked around and saw that the pros were over by the dumpster on the far side. Patrick was glad no one had been watching.

"You want to get out of here?" Teddy asked. "Like, maybe go home?"

"Fuck no," Patrick said, though his voice came out jittery. "It's cool. We're cool. We're skating, man."

Teddy nodded, but Patrick could tell he didn't really get it. Of course you fall, Patrick wanted to tell him. You fall and you get up and skate some more. But that wasn't the kind of thing you could explain to a person. You either got it or you didn't. Patrick let go of Teddy and leaned on his board. The breeze was up and he noticed shadows creeping across the skate spot. Everything had gotten darker, but maybe that was just how it felt after a fall.

"Son!" his father's voice slapped Patrick with its closeness. "What's going on here?" His father stopped running and leaned over to catch his breath.

The pros skated past just then, right when his dad was acting so lame.

"Dad," Patrick hissed.

"Christ, look at you. What happened?"

Patrick thought he saw Jamie Lawrence and the camera dude snicker and Patrick turned away from his father as fast as he could, but there was no way to make him just disappear.

"Did these fellows bother you?" his father whispered hard, his face red and still panting. "I knew you were in trouble. I saw those guys arrive and then you called and we got cut off."

"What? No. I'm fine."

"If they bothered you—"

"No one bothered me."

"So what happened?"

"I fell. It's no big deal. Really, I'm cool."

Patrick's father turned to Teddy and Teddy just shrugged.

"You look terrible," Patrick's father said. "We need to get you home and clean you up. Those cuts need antibiotic ointment. It's time to go."

No, not time to go, Patrick thought. Time to stay. Time to fucking say the thing that his father needed to hear so he'd let them stay. Patrick made his eyes go big like Teddy's and his voice went up high.

"Isn't this place awesome, Dad? See those ramps?" He nodded toward them like he was letting his father in on a secret. "These same skaters poured the concrete themselves and moved those barriers around to make it a cool spot." Patrick was pointing like crazy just to show his dad the way it was out here. "See that three-stair over there? Teddy did that today. Isn't that great?"

"I nailed it," Teddy said, standing taller.

"And over there, the nine-stair? I did it twice last week."

His father nodded a little, still not getting it.

"And that other gap, the big space next to the ledge? These guys do a huge gap like that all the time. Like it's totally normal."

His father looked at the groups of young men skating nearby. "These fellows here?"

Patrick hoped his father wouldn't point at the other skaters, and he didn't. He stepped closer to his father and talked lower now, his voice going deeper. "Those dudes are amateur skaters. They're practically pros," Patrick said.

"What does that mean exactly? Do they get paid to skateboard?"

"No, but they're sponsored by different skate companies."

"And by the skate shop downtown," Teddy chimed in. "They've got an awesome team. Patrick's definitely good enough to be on it."

Patrick watched his father closely and hoped he was starting to understand.

"And what do you get if you're sponsored?" his father asked.

He and Teddy looked at Patrick like he was some sort of expert, which Patrick had to admit he kind of was. "Free decks whenever you need one."

"And how much is a deck?"

"Fifty bucks."

"That's something."

"Shirts, shoes, stuff like that."

"Cool!" Teddy said.

"You could get Teddy a new baseball cap and me some new sneakers?" his dad asked with a smile and roughed up Teddy's hair.

Patrick swallowed. It wasn't a baseball cap if it had a skateboard logo on it. And if his father started wearing skate shoes, Patrick thought he might have to move out.

"Sure," he said, "if I'm good enough to make the team."

Then his father turned and looked at him head on. "So *are* you good enough?"

Patrick stared down at his torn shoes. After only a few weeks, rips began to appear in the same spots in every pair because he slid the same way each time he tried a trick. Hours and hours out on the driveway in the cold and then more hours in the heat of summer. Close to two years learning to do a kick-flip a few years back when he was ten. That was how long it took. He could feel a trick now in his body before he did it. He could feel it in his sleep. At the end of a good day he hurt all over, hips, legs, and back. That's what it meant to skate like he did: hours, days, weeks, months, even years. It's what he did. He skated a shitload and he loved it.

"He's super-good, Dad," Teddy said, beaming up at Patrick.

"Your mother and I have noticed you work hard at this. We're proud of you for sticking with it. You're learning important life lessons that you can apply to anything you do. Hard work pays off and important things don't come easily." He squeezed Patrick's shoulder and Patrick nodded again at the ground.

"Thanks, Dad."

"But, you know," his father continued, taking his hand away. "You can't make a living as a skateboarder and you could get seriously injured. Though it's always good to get exercise." He pulled in his stomach over his expensive belt. "But, come on, there's no point in getting too serious about all this." He stretched an arm toward the skate spot and sucked in air between his teeth in that way Patrick hated.

Patrick kept his eyes on the asphalt as it caught the light. It sparkled, as if gems were hidden beneath the surface. His dad could be such a douche. He kicked himself for ever thinking they might see things the same way. Patrick slammed the end of his board with his toe and it bounced on the concrete and popped upright. He caught it fast and held it at his side like a club.

"Skating isn't exercise, Dad. And I don't do it because it helps prepare me for something else. *This* is what I do."

His father's face froze for a moment then he let out a loud laugh. Patrick looked around to see if the other guys were watching.

"I offer you a compliment and a ride to the skate park and you give me back talk. It's time to go, young man. Your mother can deal with you."

Patrick squeezed his board to his chest and mumbled into it, "I didn't exactly want you to drive me. I could've taken the bus." His dad wouldn't know the bus didn't run on Sundays because his parents never left home and didn't know shit about the real world.

His father shook his head. "I can't wait till you outgrow this stage."

Now it was Patrick's turn to laugh. "You too, Dad."

"That's enough. Get in the car."

Patrick dropped his board and stood on it. "I'm not going."

"Oh yes, you are, and you're not coming back here, that's for damn sure."

Patrick did a kick flip right in front of his father. Then he turned and started to skate away.

"I forbid you to come here again," his father shouted after him.

"Chill out, Dad."

His father let out a long, low sound, more like a growl than anything else. "All right, then, you can get yourself home. Come on, Teddy, let's go." Patrick's father headed towards the car.

Patrick gave his father's back the finger. Then he noticed Teddy standing there. As their dad disappeared around the corner of the old warehouse, Patrick skated back to his brother and said, "Psycho, am I right?"

"You got him really mad, Patrick. You sure you don't want to come home? It's getting dark."

"No, I'm cool," Patrick said and did another kick flip. "Actually, I'm great."

"I better go." Teddy hopped onto his board and pushed to join their father. "Come home soon, OK?" he shouted back.

As Teddy slipped around the side of the warehouse, Jamie Lawrence and the camera dude skated up to Patrick. Just like that they were there beside him. All the other skaters had left by then. It was only Patrick and the hard-core guys. Let's skate all night, Patrick wanted to say, though of course he didn't.

"Hey, man," Jamie said, tossing back his hair. "Saw you eat shit earlier. You OK?"

"I'm good."

Patrick 's voice came out shaky. He coughed and hoped they hadn't heard his father being such a dick. He glanced real quick in the direction of the parking lot and wondered if maybe he should get a ride after all. The fifteen-minute car ride home would save him an hour or more of difficult skating. Patrick had to admit he didn't exactly know the way home from here.

"Listen, man," the camera dude said. "We wanted to catch you before your old man left. That was your dad, right?" Jamie asked.

Oh, shit, Patrick thought, but he had to nod.

"We should have talked to you earlier. We want to get some footage," the camera dude said.

Footage? Patrick wanted to ask.

"But it'd be good if we got, you know, parental permission since you're still a pretty young kid," Jamie said and then asked, "You *are* still a kid, right?"

What a totally weird question, Patrick thought. Wasn't it obvious he was a kid? But maybe not. Patrick nodded again.

"How old *are* you, man?" Jamie Lawrence asked.

Patrick talked to his board. "Fifteen." Might as well tell the truth, or the truth in a couple of years.

The camera dude said, "You ever land that kickflip down the gap you were trying a few weeks back?"

His heart started beating fast as it hit him that these guys had been watching him, not just today, but for a while. The blood started going wild in his head and he felt a little faint. He nodded again and knew he had to make himself talk. "Yeah."

"Sweet," Jamie Lawrence said.

"What's your name, man?" the camera dude asked.

"Patrick."

The camera dude offered a fist and Patrick lifted his, but they could see it was too messed up to bump. "You should get that cleaned up and bandaged."

"I will."

"So, like, we're filming this video, but you look so messed up, man, and now your dad's gone, we'll do it another time."

"A skate video?" Patrick's voice crackled.

"We're starting a second team with some of the younger guys," the camera dude said. "A few high-school guys. You know, your age."

No way was Patrick going to admit he was only in seventh grade. His eyes shot over to the real pro, Jamie Lawrence. With his pockmarked face and hair streaked with faded red highlights, he didn't look as good as he did in the skate videos, but Patrick supposed that was how it was. Jamie nodded at him again, but he didn't smile and Patrick was grateful. The guy wasn't treating him like anything special, because he wasn't. He was just a skater, like Jamie, just a guy who liked trashing his body day in and day out on the concrete.

"Hold on," Patrick said. "I'll go get my Dad."

"I don't know, man, you look pretty messed up," the camera dude repeated.

"I'll be right back," Patrick shouted over his shoulder, as he took off. "Don't leave!"

His legs felt super-weak and he couldn't get a full breath. His hurt knee was killing him and he could feel a trickle of blood running down his shin and pooling in his sock. The wind had picked up off the river and he was cold all over, but he rounded the building and kept on. His dad's car was still there. Patrick was suddenly psyched to tell his father and Teddy what the skaters had said, but the engine was on and the car was shifting into reverse.

"Dad!" Patrick shouted and pressed harder, pushing himself.

The car started to pull out of the parking spot as Teddy, in the backseat, turned and noticed him. His father would stop when Teddy told him Patrick was coming—but the car kept moving, driving away from Patrick and toward the exit.

"Teddy!" Patrick shouted. "Dad!"

Patrick could see Teddy lean forward and motion behind the car, his arms flailing up and down, trying to make their father stop. Finally, the brake lights went on and the shiny new car halted. His father threw open his door and stepped out. He stood on the asphalt facing Patrick with his hands on his hips. Patrick skated up fast, stopped and bent over, seriously out of breath. His legs were shaking and his hands were shaking, too. When he looked up, his dad had never seemed so big.

"Get in the car," his father said.

"I'm sorry, Dad."

"You bet you are. I need respect from you, young man. You need to think before you speak."

Patrick nodded. He picked up his board and hugged it to his chest. He was trying to think before he spoke. "Those guys," he started to say, "the pros over there—"

"I don't want to hear another word about skateboarding."

"They want me to skate with them," Patrick blurted out. "I could get sponsored. Maybe not right away, but eventually, if I skate a lot." Patrick glanced at his brother in the backseat. "And I really want to."

"No way!" Teddy called through the shut window. "That's awesome, dude!"

Patrick grinned at Teddy and Teddy grinned back—big, major grins like when they were little. But when Patrick looked back at their father, he wasn't smiling.

"Dad," Patrick said softer, but he didn't know what else to say. He'd given up trying to get his father to understand. "They need your permission to film because I'm a kid. Please, Dad?"

His father pulled back his shoulders and his chest got wider. Patrick could have sworn he was trying to look bigger and meaner than he actually was. He knew his dad wasn't a dick, not really, he just thought he should act like one.

"I don't think so. Not the way you've been behaving."

Patrick placed his skateboard down on the asphalt as if it were a fragile thing. He flicked it with the side of his foot and it rolled away from them. He stepped closer to his father and bent his head. They were practically the same height now. Patrick knew that, but it still surprised him. He wondered if maybe his father was just getting used to it, too, because he bent his head in close so their foreheads almost touched.

Patrick had this weird feeling that his dad was going to do something like hug him. Something totally dorky, though it would have been OK with him, too, so long as the older guys didn't see. But then Patrick noticed that his father's jaw muscles were bulging and his breath was still steady and fierce. His dad was still fucking furious. Patrick wasn't sure he'd ever seen him that way before and it made him wonder if maybe he was wrong about his dad. Maybe this was who he really was, deep down. This guy with the hard face and the mean eyes that stared right through you. He looked not just cool, but cold, totally cold, like he didn't give a shit about anything or anyone else, not even his son.

Patrick sensed an awesome gap opening up between them there on the asphalt. He recognized the feeling in his gut as he looked across the space. The distance was frightening, but there was no way around it. The truth was, you wrecked yourself more times than not. You didn't make it some days, but you had no choice but to try again the next day.

Patrick searched for something to say to his dad that would turn things around and tighten the gap. He wanted him to understand so bad. He knew he had to go for it and not quit until he had done it right. The only way was to bend your knees low, square your shoulders to the ground, and propel yourself upwards. You launched from wherever it was you had started and whoever it was you had been. Every trick tore a hole in the sky and carried you into a bright pocket of air. He told his body, his legs, his whole being to take him across to the other side. It was time to show his father how it was done.

New Year's Day

The afternoon was unseasonably warm and the family had only the screen door to protect them, and it was unlocked. The local newspaper headlines called it the New Year's Day Massacre. A couple in their late thirties and their two daughters, ages six and four, were murdered in their basement. Though the article did not describe the deaths, by the following afternoon, Jessica, and just about everyone else in town, knew it had been gruesome.

Such a heinous act was only made worse by taking place on a day set aside for reflection or renewed hope or at least some relaxation. An uneasy sadness settled over the town. The coming year looked bleak. The day, which had started out mild and overcast, ended with a peaceful drizzle, but Jessica couldn't get warm.

The papers reported that the murderer had set fire to the house after the crime. A neighbor had smelled the smoke, had gone onto the front porch and called through the screen. Getting no response, he stepped inside to investigate. Everyone tried to imagine how that must have felt: to walk into a smoldering house, calling out the names of your friends, and hearing nothing in response. You search around and finally stumble on the bodies.

The town knew the man who had discovered the crime. They knew the dead husband's colleagues from the high school where he taught. The wife's helpers at the small consignment shop she owned out on the byway. The two little girls' teachers and babysitters. The family had lived here all their lives. If you didn't know them yourself, Jessica thought, you knew someone who did. She shuddered to think that one of the daughters could have been a student in her class if the family had lived in her same school district.

Despite the District Attorney putting a gag on the case, the town reeled with questions and rumors. Was there something shady about the parents that had led to this— drugs or sex or something sinister no one could even imagine? People close to them were brought in for questioning. Everyone knew it was routine, still it made them wonder. The couple had no immediate family, no elderly parents out of town, no siblings or cousins in counties nearby. Did that suggest something? No one wanted to think these things—certainly Jessica didn't— but that was how it was in those first weeks.

Vigils took place outside the house and a memorial service was held. Days passed, children went back to school, the first snow fell and business resumed, though not at the mother's shop, which stood unchanged month after month with no relatives to claim it or help out and the small staff of college girls too upset to even try. Everyone wanted to move on, to get over it, but didn't know how. Neighborhood meetings were held. A detective talked to the citizens about safety and future precautions. They locked their doors now and assumed that was how it had to be from now on.

In those first weeks, Jessica spotted mothers whispering to each other in the grocery store aisles out of earshot of their young children. She saw a teenage girl crying on her boyfriend's shoulder in the parking lot. At school drop-off, she noticed mothers and fathers giving their children longer than usual hugs before saying goodbye.

She lived alone in the next neighborhood over from the crime. As she stood washing her dishes at the sink after supper, she had taken to staring out at the patch of backyard. Shrubs planted by previous owners had filled in nicely, creating a perfect border around the rectangle of lawn. This was her first home, bought with help from her father and her savings from teaching. The previous spring she had brought in blooming boughs from her own azaleas to her kindergarteners. But, now, in mid-winter, she stood with her eyes fixed to the ragged outline. She knew there was nothing out there behind those bushes. Still, she stood waiting, sensing the possibility that someone could at any moment step onto the grass.

Jessica had grown up in a town a lot like this one, only smaller. She had never seen a horror movie or even a thriller and was uneasy about detective films, but her grandmother had scared her when she was small with stories of hell. As an adult she knew that old-fashioned fire and brimstone was meant to trick the ignorant. Still, some cloud of those Bible lessons hung over Jessica, although she had always done her best to maintain a firm stance against such creeping darkness.

She had been perky and bright as a girl, intent on bringing nothing but good cheer to others. Since high school she had volunteered at the hospital and took meals to the homebound. She was active at her church, a progressive Presbyterian congregation where the minister had no intention of coercing you into heaven. She couldn't recall anyone even mentioning hell, until the crime on New Year's Day.

If asked, Jessica would have argued that the world was a beautiful place and the people in it good. She didn't believe this out of naiveté—viscerally she sensed that the world was a terrible place—but as an act of defiance. She would be damned if the awful things that were always happening in the newspaper would get to her. Her life had been dominated by good fortune and that seemed worth preserving to balance out the misery that existed elsewhere.

Though no one would have known it from looking at her—an adored teacher, a strong community member, a homeowner with a steady boyfriend, Wayne, whom she had met at church, a success in all the right ways at only age twenty-eight—Jessica kept her upright posture in an effort to resist the relentless tug of despair that she knew threatened to swirl us all into its vortex at any moment. She embraced her father's often repeated, cheery directives of "stiff upper lip" and "pull up your socks." For Jessica, they offered resistance against a current that could first weaken, then ruin you, if you weren't careful.

This evening, as she washed and rinsed her plate and mug, she could not seem to step away from the window. Something might be out there that could not be ignored. It took the phone ringing to break the spell. She dropped the sponge, wiped her hands on the dishtowel and dug her cell phone out of her back pocket.

The voice of one of her church friends crashed out at her. Jessica held the phone away from her ear as Cynthia shouted: "Reverend Tim approved and the Executive Committee authorized the matching funds! Watch out, New York, here we come!"

"Fantastic!" Jessica tried to match her friend's exuberance.

"I bet we even have enough in the Contemporary Service's kitty to cover a Broadway show. Between now and April we can pull together at least one major fundraiser to help out with the airfare. I was thinking, how about a

"New York, New York" evening? Potluck desserts, games, or a raffle and cake walk, or is that just too old-fashioned? Unless we decide to make it an old-fashioned evening? You know, New York in the 1890s? I bet Richard over at the Costume Shop would donate dresses. The guys could wear spats. All right, Jimmy would wear spats. Can't you just picture it? You wouldn't believe how much a well-run cake walk brings in."

Jessica searched around in a kitchen drawer, found a pen, and on the back of a Chinese take-out menu she began to jot a few notes as she and Cynthia brainstormed. Together they would organize the trip, using the services of a local travel agent—Margaret Johansen out by the Shoprite, crackerjack at this sort of thing. Fundraising would be relatively easy, given the level of interest. With good publicity, new people would join the Contemporary Service gang. Jessica cited "Growing the Congregation" and "Helping People Take Their Minds Off Things" as their "Two Principal Goals."

"You don't think it's too soon, do you?" Jessica found herself asking when Cynthia finally took a breath, though she knew it was more a question for their minister than for someone as full-speed-ahead as her friend.

"No, it's a good thing. Time we got back on our horse, and what better way to do that than in New York City?"

"And Reverend Tim actually approves?"

"He said A-OK."

"I'm just concerned."

"Well, of course you're concerned. We're all concerned, more than concerned. We've been scared silly, is what we've been. I think New York in spring is just what the doctor ordered. I'll take one of those horse and buggy rides through Central Park if it's the last thing I do. It's crazy not to have been there before. Life is too short."

Both women paused at that thought.

"I've never been there either," Jessica confessed.

"Jimmy certainly has, the nut. He saves up every year for his annual Bacchanalia, as he calls it. I think he might have a special friend up there, if you know what I mean."

Jessica didn't exactly, but let Cynthia continue.

"How about we put a little poll down on the trip application asking if they've been before—not that it's any of our business, but it'd be fun to know, wouldn't it?"

Jessica marked that down. Cynthia was the idea person while Jessica was strong on follow-through and the nitty-gritty details of getting things done. In the following days their committee planned two bake sales, a spring bulb sale, a CD swap with an entrance fee and, of course, the big event to be held in the Social Hall. Every night for weeks, Jessica was either out at a meeting or on the phone for hours with various women making plans. She hardly had a moment to stand at her kitchen window or wander around in her home at night wondering if she'd ever feel secure again.

She supposed she had Cynthia to thank for that, although strangely, she almost missed the melancholy, the worrisome sadness that had hovered over her in the days following the murders. She had started to feel comfortable being so full of doubt, as if this unsettled period was proving to her what she had always suspected: a dark cloud spread over absolutely everything, making Jessica wonder how she had missed it before. She didn't, however, miss the accompanying fear. Now, when she hit the bed at night, she had no energy left to picture what must have happened in that basement or embellish new versions with herself as victim.

The night before the big evening, she and the other women and Jimmy gathered at Cynthia's house to try on the costumes donated by the Costume Shop. They stayed past eleven making decorations, pushing silver thumbtacks into Styrofoam balls to hang from the ceiling and twirling fabric for swags. Jimmy had decided to cut costs by using plain kitchen cellophane with black nylon stockings from thrift stores around town (crotches and toes cut out), although the others thought he was mad for not just buying silver and black fabric at JoAnn's. In the end, he proved the women wrong, and the long, sheer braids looked smashing.

At one point in the evening, Jessica found herself alone with Jimmy in the kitchen, refilling the snack plates and preparing a fresh pot of coffee. He was a skinny young man with a lightly acned face and hair spiked unnaturally and (could it be?) frosted at the tips. Even his eyes were unlike any of the men around here: they had none of the pragmatic dullness, but instead sparkled. Although he was only a few years younger than Jessica, he somehow made her feel like a matron, someone already settled in her ways. They had been in choir together for years, but had never really gotten to know one another, though she had noticed that his good cheer was contagious over in his section. The tenors were always cutting up and getting into trouble. It had made her wish she could sing lower.

Now she sensed that the two of them worked well in the kitchen together, something that was not true of all her friends. They danced around one another, she in the 1890's floor-length evening dress, and he in khakis and a top hat. They took down Cynthia's mugs from the cabinet, located the sugar and cream set, slid cookies off the cookie sheets from the oven—all with grace and ease. Jessica laughed when he pirouetted, coffee pot in hand. He was something. She took out the one-percent milk and was about to fill the creamer when he grabbed the carton from her hand.

"Let's give them a little treat, shall we?" he asked before flinging it back into the refrigerator and pulling out the half and half instead. "Everyone needs to live it up now and then."

He spun away, taking the ladies their coffee and cookies. The living room was so bright and nicely decorated, the banter of the women lively and fun, but still, Jessica found herself turning away and looking out Cynthia's window at the wide expanse of yard that led down to an apple orchard at the back of the property. The moonlight struck one side of each tree in the distance, making the scene appear more like an unfinished drawing of trees than the thing itself. Jessica considered whether she felt worried at the sight. Did she picture someone dangerous walking up from the pasture? She let out a sigh and leaned against the counter. The fact that she had to ask herself if she was afraid made her realize she had come some distance in the past three weeks.

Then Jimmy was there again, leaning at her elbow.

"You look lovely in that Isabel Archer getup."

"Who's that? Some New York designer no one knows about around here except you?"

"Never mind," he said, patting her hand. "Isn't it too bad we can't dress like this all the time? I poured us some coffee." He handed her a mug.

"It'll keep me up."

"We're not even a thousand thumbtacks into the project yet. Drink away."

Jessica looked past Jimmy and out at the back lawn again. He followed her gaze, pressing into the counter beside her.

"If it weren't for the orchards and the ponds and the fields," he said, "I wouldn't live out here in the sticks. I just love being so close to the mountains, don't you? I go up there all the time."

"Me, too."

"But," he said with an exaggerated sigh, "looks like I have to leave it all behind if I'm ever to be happy."

"What do you mean?" she asked, turning to him. "Why can't you be happy here?"

"Oh, honey, the idea of a guy like me being really happy in this town is absurd and everyone knows it."

Jessica's cheeks flushed and she let out a high laugh, which she quickly contained.

"I've been trying to convince a certain someone to move, but no way. It's just too small and provincial for us. No offense. This country boy has to pack his bags and head to the big city."

Jessica was saddened at the thought of losing Jimmy just when they were becoming friends. But what bothered her more was a different, insistent reality she had never let herself consider before. She wished that Jimmy and his mysterious partner could settle down as full members of the community in their small town. She was happy for him that he'd found someone, but thought it terrible that he was being forced to move not because of a job, but because they didn't fit in. His predicament struck her as an awful truth, one that could no longer be ignored. Of course he must be miserable, she realized, although he appeared so lighthearted all the time. He rested his chin on his folded hands now and leaned over the counter.

Jessica summoned up a chipper voice and said, "Now look at us, a couple of sad sacks."

"Not me." He grinned at her.

"Well, me neither."

But their gazes drifted again out the back window.

After a long moment, Jessica whispered, "It's hard not to think about it. I just don't know if I'm really ready. Cynthia keeps saying it's time to get back on our horses."

Jimmy snorted. Jessica leaned toward him ever so slightly, their shoulders grazing.

"I've been imagining something like that happening all my life," he said, his voice soft and conspiratorial.

"Then it finally does happen, but to a normal, run-of-the-mill family."

Jessica set down her mug. "You've imagined something like this before?" Her voice contained both shock and its opposite, a sudden understanding.

He pushed back from the counter. "Wouldn't you, if you were me?"

Jessica didn't know what to say. She'd never had a conversation like this before in her life. And while it made her uneasy, she also felt an excited tingling down her arms. The hardened look on his face helped her contain a shiver. Of course, he would imagine such awful things. He was one of the people she might read about in the newspaper, a stranger with terrible luck. It made her wonder who else she knew like this. Or if it was true that any of us could be struck down by the awfulness of things at any moment and for no apparent reason. Maybe that was the real lesson of New Year's Day.

Friday morning, January 22nd, Jessica hurried down her front walk in her bathrobe and the new Christmas slippers from her mother. She was alone. Wayne had gone home the night before because of the special needs kids' basketball tournament he had to referee that morning. Jessica swooped down, picked up the newspaper and scurried back inside. A cold snap had finally hit, wilting the rhododendrons under the front windows. Her coffee was ready in the new machine from Wayne. She poured herself a mug and sat down at her tidy kitchen table, spreading out the paper before her.

The murderers had been captured in Florida. The story was there below the blazing headlines. Jessica lifted the paper closer and read as quickly as she could, skimming the first paragraph, which restated the crime, as if there was anyone in this town who didn't know already.

Two strangers, men from a large city three hundred
miles away, had been passing through, high on something
terrible that resulted in the violent outburst. No reason
behind it, no cause. They had stopped their truck outside
the house with the open door. There was no purpose
behind them being in that neighborhood or getting off
the highway in the first place. Jessica looked up and
wondered: couldn't they have just kept driving?

She read on. And there it was in print for the first time:
a statement of what everyone had sensed by now, despite
the discreetness of the detectives. The family, all four, had
been bound, gagged, beaten, their throats slashed. Jessica
took in a quick breath. The crime was unfathomable.
There was no explanation for it, unless you believed in
evil—unmitigated, indiscriminate evil. She felt oddly
relieved, not by its existence, but by her willingness to
finally let down her guard and accept it openly.

Yet, knowing who had done the crime brought her
little immediate relief. The story made no sense. They
might now know the who and the how, but not the why.
Jessica suspected there would never be any knowing it.

She could imagine the day too well: the mother had
been in the kitchen making lunch. Jessica's eyes stung as
she envisioned the woman heating a can of soup and
grilling cheese sandwiches for her family. She could
picture the father and the younger daughter down in the
basement adjusting the seat on her new Christmas tricycle
when the mother heard footsteps on the front porch. She
would have hurried to see if it was their older child, the
six-year-old, come home from her first sleepover, a special
New Year's Eve night away at her new best friend's house.
But—here Jessica pressed herself to try to believe it—
instead of finding her daughter, she found two men
standing at the door. They would have forced the mother
to the basement to join the father and younger daughter.

No one knew what happened next, the paper said, although the trial would undoubtedly shed more light. Jessica took a sip of coffee and pressed onward. Although a part of her didn't want to consider any of this, she had to know more, had to know it all.

Sometime later, perhaps only a short time, the older daughter returned from her sleepover. The mother of the new best friend came to the screen door to drop off the girl and, not knowing the family well (the girls were friends from school, not the neighborhood), rang the bell. The mother was sent up from the basement.

Then, Jessica read more slowly, deliberately, as if searching each word for the truth. The other mother had stood at the screen door and offered a few pleasantries about the successful sleepover. She noticed that the mother of the doomed family looked pale, perhaps ill, so she asked if she was all right. The mother said she wasn't feeling well, probably too much New Year's Eve. The other mother offered to keep the little girl and her sister for the afternoon, so the parents could rest. But, the mother said, no, they would manage. The little girl asked where her sister was and the mother motioned to the basement. Both mothers then watched as the little girl scampered down the hall to the top of the steps, turned back to thank the other mother for the sleepover, and disappeared down the stairs.

Jessica reread the paragraph. Then read it again. She noticed the words blurring before her eyes and pressed hot tears from her lashes. Her hand trembled as she read it one more time. Then she bowed her head, letting it drop between her knees, the soft terry cloth of the bathrobe caressing her cheek. She breathed in through her nose and out her mouth as she had been taught in CPR class at the hospital. Slowly, the blackness that had been filling the edges of her vision receded. It was a long while before she lifted her head.

How had those two mothers let the little girl go down those basement stairs? How was it that the doomed mother could not make some signal? Mouth 911 or put a finger to her own temple? Couldn't she have whispered the word "help"? And why wasn't the other mother, the mother of the daughter's friend, more attentive, more aware? How could she have been so oblivious to the terrible thing happening right before her eyes? Jessica's head was reeling with questions.

She slowly stood and took her mug to the sink, poured out the rest of her coffee and started going at it with a sponge. The crime was one thing. They had all had weeks to consider the crime. But this other business, this story of the two mothers, was what troubled Jessica now: two women standing on the threshold of the house, the screen door propped open, the girl standing between them. Jessica could picture it: the gray day outside, the soup and grilled cheese sandwiches growing cold on the kitchen counter. The criminals must have threatened the mother that if she said anything, hinted at anything, they would kill her husband and younger daughter downstairs. But couldn't the two women have silently conveyed something? Jessica set the mug in the empty dish-drainer.

Couldn't they, for once, have stopped pretending that everything was all right?

She splashed water on her face. She had never used the kitchen sink for this purpose before, but instead preferred the proper cleansers and lotions upstairs. She pulled out a dishtowel and began scrubbing her wet cheeks. She took up the bar of soap from its dish by the sink and covered her face with suds. The towel was coarse, the soap unpleasant, and the water too hot, but Jessica kept on.

Perhaps the doomed mother had said nothing for fear that the other mother, a virtual stranger but a mother after all, would have been taken into the basement, too? That was heroic, Jessica conceded, but somehow, she still couldn't forgive the murdered woman for not letting out even a peep. It was terrible, Jessica realized, to find fault with someone so victimized, yet here she was—hating the two women for their ineffectualness, their weakness.

Jessica rinsed for the final time, water dripping from her chin. Would she have been courageous enough or smart enough to do something different? Jessica had to ask herself: would she have seen what was right in front of her face?

Everything seemed to rankle Jessica leading up to the big event. What did Cynthia mean by Jimmy's annual Bacchanalia in New York? And just how miserable was he? The questions led to other ones about the crime. She couldn't shake the image of the two women at the screen door of the house. She kept replaying the scene in her mind, but the outcome was always the same. What could they have done? What would she have done? And now, the troubling question of what it was like to be Jimmy in this town.

Somehow these thoughts compounded into the question everyone must ask themselves at some point: what would she have done in the Holocaust? Jessica was ashamed to realize that she'd never pressed herself to think about it before. But, in the endless sleepless hours the previous night, she had tried to truly consider it, even though she couldn't, not really. She assumed she'd have done the right thing, maybe even the heroic thing, although in her bleary, predawn state, she wondered if that was true at all.

The birds had started in the darkness, heckling and mocking her with their racket. Finally, as daylight softened the sill and spiders of frost glistened on the winter lawn,

Jessica turned away from the window and prepared for the school day ahead. The crisp weather seemed to signal a new start and even the possibility of forgiveness, but Jessica would have none of that. She sensed that a disturbing haze would continue to shroud her on this of all days.

She left work early that afternoon for the first time in four years, asking her assistant to take over at naptime, clean up, and dismissal. Everyone assumed she was exhausted from the church event preparations. They advised her to go home and take a nap before the big night. She didn't. Instead, Jessica cleaned out her kitchen cabinets and organized her linen closet. When Wayne called at five o'clock to say he was coming over to pick her up, she begged off. She needed more time to get into the costume dress, while he was needed over at the Social Hall to hang the last of the decorations. She would be along shortly.

Jessica spent considerable time in the bath and afterward used every lotion and cream she had. She pulled on the satin and taffeta gown, but had a hard time with the zipper low in the back. She looked at herself in the mirror and was surprised to see that she looked stunning, her hair up in lovely wisps, her face flushed and pretty. She could take little pleasure in the sight. Her hands trembled so much she barely managed to shut the clasp on her ruby pendant.

She told herself it was only excitement about the upcoming event. She tried to push the frantic questions about the crime from her mind. And the more and more undeniable thought that she would have done the same thing as the two mothers. To calm herself, she tried instead to worry about Jimmy. At least she could try to do something about Jimmy. About herself she wasn't as sure.

In the end, Jessica arrived only fifteen minutes late, her clipboard in hand. Cynthia looked wonderful, the extensions woven into her bob at the salon well worth the splurge. Wayne was startlingly handsome in his tux. He couldn't stop fawning over Jessica, but in a nice way, pulling out the seat for her at the registration desk and fussing with the curls fallen over her bare shoulders. As he handed her a paper cup brimming with pink punch, she told herself she would be selfish not to have a good time.

Attendance was better than they could have hoped. The women looked terrific in their costumes, even if some dressed in sequined flapper minis and others were done up like Scarlett O'Hara. Over at the roulette wheel, Reverend Tim was raking in the chips and laughing hard, so unlike the ministers at the more traditional churches. Jessica couldn't imagine anyone coming here and not wanting to join their fun congregation. The potluck desserts were extravagant, some right out of *Gourmet* magazine and *Martha Stewart*. Even the decorations seemed bright and sophisticated under the glaring lights of the social hall.

Forty-five minutes into the festivities, Jessica decided she could close up registration and join in. She was snapping shut the petty cash box and putting the key into her bra (how did those women manage back then?) when a couple arrived who Jessica had never seen before. She took their money and welcomed them. They seemed nice, though quiet. Jessica felt pleased that Cynthia's and her little idea was now bringing together absolute strangers. It had to be good for the town. She chided herself for questioning the timing of the event. The husband of the couple put down their names on the sign-in sheet and they drifted into the party, tentative, more watchers than the partying type.

Jessica stacked up the trip flyers, cash box, pens, and nametags. She glanced at the sign-up sheets and, just out of curiosity, read the new couple's names so she might address them familiarly and help them feel more at home. "Colin and Molly Wilson," it said in a tiny scrawl. *Molly Wilson!* Jessica recognized the name from the newspaper: the woman who had dropped off the older daughter on New Year's Day.

She looked across to where they stood apart from the crowd, still in their coats, though the rack was in plain sight to the right of the entrance. Jessica's fist tightened around the pen in her hand. Why couldn't they just go on in, she thought? They should stop staring from the sidelines, making everyone else uncomfortable. Although, truthfully, she had to admit, no one had yet noticed the Wilsons. Before she had a chance to think twice, she had set down the pen and marched over to them, the taffeta of her dress making a ruckus as she came.

"Let me take your coats," she said, and started to peel Colin's coat off his sloped shoulders. He shimmied out of it reluctantly, his prematurely bald head bobbing as he thanked her.

"We're all right," he mumbled. "Not sure how long we can stay, really."

Jessica had his scarf now and was starting to go for Molly's drab three-quarter-length quilted parka. At least she hadn't worn it on New Year's Day, Jessica thought. It would have been too heavy for that mild afternoon. Molly slipped out of the coat and undid the knitted scarf from around her neck. It was striped in mismatched colors, unblocked knitting, something imperfect that a child might make. She wore a basic skirt and cardigan outfit, more like work clothes really, no jewelry, just flats. Her husband wore a sweatshirt, for goodness sake, Jessica thought. No effort to dress up, no attempt to fit in or get over it and move on.

She swirled away with their coats in her arms. As she hung them up on the last few coat hangers, she tried to tell herself to calm down, to not be so upset with this woman. Still, she could feel herself burning up and not just from the weight of the coats. She wanted to say something, felt determined to, but what?

When she turned around again, Molly was standing alone. Her husband had slouched off toward the refreshments. Good, Jessica thought, they were making an effort. She saw Jimmy in his red vest, top hat and spats behind the soda and punch bar and somehow wished she could send him a message via telepathy: make that man's drink a strong one, she'd say. Put something in it to wash away a person's memory and make them feel whole again. Or maybe concoct a drink to make a person disappear altogether.

Wouldn't that have been easier, Jessica thought, to have just given in and gone down into the basement with the family and gotten it over with, instead of having to live out the rest of your life standing on the outside as Molly did now? The woman would never recover from it. The shadow of that day and her decision, or lack of decision, or human blindness, or simply bad luck, would hang over her forever. How could Molly forgive herself, if Jessica was having such a hard time and she hadn't even been there? How could this woman live with herself? Jessica wanted to know, because she could never have done it herself.

Jessica edged up beside Molly and forced a smile. She knew she looked beautiful in her period dress and the other woman blushed slightly as if she were standing next to a movie star.

"Lovely dress," Molly said.

"It's from over at the Costume Shop."

Molly nodded.

"I like your—" Jessica started, but hadn't thought it through. "Your scarf. Nice and warm."

"Yes, it is."

They watched the couples at the roulette wheel and others ogling the desserts. "You and your husband must buy a raffle ticket for the prize dessert."

"Oh, I don't think so. We can't stay long."

"That's too bad," Jessica said, letting her voice fall to a whisper. "I suppose it's difficult getting out and socializing these days?"

Molly didn't flinch, didn't take her eyes off her husband, who was ordering drinks from Jimmy all the way across the social hall.

"I've been trying to imagine," Jessica started, but then stopped. The husband was turning now and heading back across the room, two full plastic cups in his hands. Jessica tried to hurry her thoughts. She would have wanted more time alone with Molly, hours really, perhaps days. "I've had to wonder," she blurted out, "what was it like that morning?"

"Oh, no," Molly whispered without looking at Jessica, "well, thank you." She stepped toward her husband.

Jessica bustled beside her, brushing back her swishing skirt from the other woman's legs. "I mean, I've tried to understand how she could have let her daughter go down those stairs," she almost shouted, unable to control herself. "I've been asking myself how that could have happened. Didn't you sense something? Weren't you aware of anything? It just doesn't seem possible—"

"We have to go now," Molly said to her husband, her body beginning to tremble. She whipped around and headed in the direction of the coat rack.

"I see," Colin said. Flustered, he placed the cups in Jessica's hands. "She's still not well," he added, more to himself than to her, then raced after his wife, gathered up their coats, and in a moment, they were gone.

Jessica stood staring at the leather-backed doors of the social hall as they swung shut. Her cheeks were burning and sweat slipped down her tightly corseted ribs. Her hands shook and the ginger ale sloshed over its rim. She had never been so rude and cruel to anyone in her life. And yet she could barely keep herself from chasing after the woman, hounding her, pounding on the windows of her car and shouting. Jessica realized she herself really was a despicable person. Truly, she was.

She turned and raced across the hall to Jimmy, vaguely aware of Wayne trying to catch her eye from his spot at the bingo table. She pressed her way around the drink table, her skirt knocking a stack of unused plastic cups to the floor.

"Jimmy," she said. "Help."

"At your service," he said brightly as he handed a soda to an elderly gentleman.

"Always hop to it when a lady calls," the man winked before stepping away.

Jessica took hold of Jimmy's arm and yanked him after her.

"Don't tell me Reverend Tim's been caught embezzling at the poker table," Jimmy said.

Suddenly choked with tears, Jessica said, "She was here. The woman who dropped off the little girl that morning."

It took a moment, but then Jimmy's face registered the horror she hoped it might. She knew he would understand.

"Did you talk to her?"

"I hounded her. I was absolutely awful. I was cruel and horrid. I chased her from the party."

"You did?" Jimmy said, smiling nervously in disbelief, but worried as well.

"It isn't funny."

"No, no, it isn't." He put his arm around her and whisked her through the swinging doors to the kitchen.

"I tormented that woman." Jessica broke into sobs. "That poor, undeserving woman." She threw her arms around him.

Jimmy held her gingerly and Jessica nuzzled her cheek against his bony shoulder.

"Dear, miserable Jessica," he said as her tears darkened his vest.

Although she wondered if he were mocking her, she had no choice but to let herself go. Much to her astonishment, Jessica felt in that moment that Jimmy was the one person in their town who could understand her.

Springtime, New York! April 4-7. Only this year, a freezing rain had started before their flight arrived and kept them circling LaGuardia an extra forty-five minutes. They missed the first item on their itinerary altogether, a Circle Line Cruise around Manhattan: all for the best because the wind off the Hudson had turned icy and the ladies had brought only spring coats.

Cynthia insisted on taking her buggy ride that first afternoon, so the willing ones piled under coarse wool blankets borrowed from the horse cabbie, blew warm breath on their hands as they rolled through Central Park. Jimmy, seated beside Cynthia, wouldn't stop whispering about what usually took place under those blankets. Jessica leaned into Wayne and focused on the clip clop of the horse's hooves on pavement. The thin lacquer of ice on the branches of the cherry trees appeared slick and elegant, very New York, and the dusting of snow on the blossoms made them look like costly confections. That springtime had already come weeks before to their hometown made this second chilly spring all the more fanciful.

By the afternoon of their second day, the weather had shifted and a mild breeze brushed Jessica and Wayne forward as they walked happily hand in hand up Madison Avenue. They stopped before the windows of the shops to ogle the haute couture, but would never have wanted to go inside. The restaurants were as fantastic as everyone had always said—dinner at a wood-paneled steakhouse their first night and sushi the next. Their hotel was more of a disappointment, but what could you expect from a chain? And Cynthia snored, which she had failed to mention. But by the second night, they were feeling more settled, less awestruck by the city. They knew the nearest pharmacy and had ridden the subway twice. It was remarkable how quickly a person could adapt to a new environment, Jessica thought. She could almost imagine living here, if it weren't so completely out of the question.

And then, all too soon, the trip was almost over. On their last night, after an exhausting day of museums and a quick supper at one of Famous Ray's pizzerias, a plan was made to meet in the lobby at seven before taking cabs or the subway to theaters around town. (They had seen *Cats* the night before, which Jessica considered quite strange, though she had kept that to herself for fear that she had missed something.) Some of their gang was too pooped and had decided to stay in for their last night. They would join the Reverend up in his suite for some pinochle. Wayne had caught a cold on their first afternoon on the carriage ride and had valiantly held off collapsing ever since, but there was no question now that he needed to crawl into bed and sleep. Cynthia and the others were intent on another big Broadway production, but Jessica and Jimmy had had enough of the big shows. So it turned out that they were on their own—if such a thing were possible in New York City.

They set out to see a play Jimmy had picked up cheap tickets for: a production of *Hedda Gabler* at a downtown off-off Broadway theater. Jessica remembered hearing of the play in high school, although she had never read or seen it. The theater was in a cramped little space on a side street in the West Village, a neighborhood Jimmy seemed to know well. They passed several groups of men milling around and Jessica wondered if that made Jimmy feel comfortable—to be not so terribly different for once. She almost felt she could ask him, that was how close they had become in the previous weeks, but she was trying to stay light and not be "a drag," as he had taken to playfully calling her.

They took their seats in a row of fold-up chairs and settled in for the show. It was long, with several intermissions. Jessica did not move from her seat once. She had never seen anything like it, with that terrible woman at the center of the story ruining the lives of everyone around her. She felt indignant toward Hedda and yet also, in her heart, feared that she was not so dissimilar. When Jimmy went off to the men's room, Jessica let herself recall how she had treated Molly Wilson at the social hall. Heat rose up her cheeks as if the moment had just taken place. She herself was every bit as cruel as this Hedda character, every bit as shameful and selfish.

When the play finally ended with that shocking bang of the pistol offstage and the realization that Hedda had killed herself, Jessica couldn't help but gasp. Luckily the applause covered it. She was among the first to stand, offering a robust ovation. She had an urgent need to go to the rest room, her bottom had pins and needles from so much sitting, and her eyes were leaking tears of outrage, yet she was still the last to stop clapping.

Outside on the sidewalk, she hugged Jimmy and thanked him, though she worried that the play had somehow changed her life and not necessarily for the better. In her crowded mind, she wondered, among other things, if Wayne deserved someone else, someone more innocent and kind, and if she would make him miserable in time.

"A solid production," Jimmy said. "I'd give it a eight out of ten."

Jessica could hardly believe he sounded so unfazed.

"Fantastic *Mommie Dearest* Hedda. And that Lovborg was quite the jilted lover, wasn't he?"

She didn't really understand his comments, but nodded along as they wound their way up the sidewalk toward the Christopher Street subway stop. Jessica was too absorbed to consider the play as merely a story. What she wanted to talk to Jimmy about was something larger. She wanted to talk to Jimmy about life.

"I've seen that Hedda before," he was saying. "He used to do *Mame*, I think. Too bad he didn't get to use his voice in this one. If I remember right, he has quite a baritone."

Jessica stopped cold, straining to see Jimmy's expression in the streetlight.

"You look so cute," he said, "all bundled up." He hitched up the collar of her coat. "Let's get back to the hotel. I couldn't be more exhausted."

Jessica's head was spinning as Jimmy took her arm. *A man* had played Hedda Gabler? How had she missed that? It was bad enough that the play itself had gone into her gut and wrenched it inside out, but now this. She hadn't even realized what she'd been looking at for three hours.

"I didn't know," she said, her voice rising with her tears. "I didn't see it."

"Oh, honey," Jimmy said, "let's get you back home before your head explodes."

As he walked her down the subway steps, Jessica reached for his hand. It was thin-boned and cold and in the subterranean light she noticed, not for the first time, his badly bitten nails and raw cuticles. She wanted to cry out at the painful sight. It was all so awful, and yet he was also so wonderful. She lifted Jimmy's hand up to her lips and kissed it hard and with great feeling.

"Oh, Jimmy," she said, "I love you. Everyone does."

He let out a laugh, clapped his arm around her shoulder, and gave her a squeeze in return. "Take it easy, sweetheart. It's going to be all right."

Jessica had assumed all along that the mother went back down into the basement out of fear or a plan that went badly awry, but now a new thought came rushing at her as violently as the train approaching them in the station. What if the mother who had died didn't have a clue what she was doing, but simply didn't want to be separated from her family? In the midst of her panic and pain, that was all that she knew. Jessica could imagine feeling that way now, lost and without hope, and yet hoping nonetheless.

And maybe Molly—miserable, plain Molly—had been nothing more than an unsuspecting person, no more blind or ignorant than most. Yet that woman was saddled now and forever with the inescapable, human knowledge that she could have, should have, seen and known more, done more. But wasn't that true of us all? Because even though there was indeed a hell, Jessica felt certain of that now, there was also a heaven, and here on earth we strained toward it every day, each in our own way.

A tremor of recognition ran down her spine as she looked around at the subway platform with new eyes. That the station was crowded with people out and about past midnight seemed remarkable to her. So many things were remarkable, or terrible, or both. She felt grateful to Jimmy for holding her hand and positioning them in the right place for when the train would arrive. She could hear its rumble and feel the air starting to stir at its approach. Jessica wondered what they were all doing up so late. Where were they going? What did they do in their lives? *Who, in fact, were they?* As she held tight to Jimmy's hand, she realized she very much wanted to know.

Easter Morning

We came carrying platters of foods to suit the season: asparagus, frittatas, homemade bread, and for dessert, carrot cupcakes with tiny frosting carrots that one of us mothers had stayed up past midnight to perfect. For the children, we had filled gaudy plastic eggs with treasure: shiny silver bells, pieces of colored glass, whistles, and shells. Now they hunted through the ivy and up the garden paths as we watched with pride, knowing that after all we had done, all we had managed, nothing could be lost on us—for we saw the children and the hidden eggs and the narrowing distance between them.

We had set out folding tables under the longed-for April sun and now we counted our blessings this Easter morning not in prayer, but with each bite taken and story told. The fathers talked about nothing really—vacations and the cutting of shrubs with electric tools, telling jokes on themselves as both heroes and sidekicks. They chuckled in pale sunlight while we women huddled around the food, arranging the dishes we had brought, and whispering about a car accident that had almost taken one of these families earlier that winter.

The car had spun out of control on black ice in another

state, causing it to flip and land beneath a highway bridge. The husband had broken his collarbone and several ribs, while the toddler had a broken arm, and the mother a punctured lung. Pinned to the ceiling, she had silently begged each passing car on the road above to notice them in the dark below. Long, dangerous minutes passed as they waited in the upside down car in the freezing rain for someone to come. Then the young child noticed that their dog was missing and let out a loud, shrill cry the likes of which the mother had never heard before. It was the cry that saved them. Soon, sirens rang out.

But that wasn't the only miracle. The dog had jumped out on impact and run away. There had been no sign of him until just a few days before this gathering when a phone call came from a couple back in the other state. This family, our friends, drove all that way back to that frightful place to retrieve the pet that now stood beside the mother, its tail wagging at the scents of food. The dog seemed infinitely patient as it waited for scraps to fall.

"He lived an altogether different life," the mother said, looking down at him by her side. "Can you imagine? The children think it's normal to disappear like that and then return, but what are the chances?"

She didn't wipe away the tears that had stalled at the corners of her eyes. We stood listening, then reached for her elbow and handed her a paper cup of punch. Each of us wondered if the rumors about her husband threatening to leave her were true. Perhaps the whole family would up and move to another state and start a new life. It was hard to guess and impossible to ask, but we knew that the tears weren't only for the returned dog.

The children then came running, Easter baskets banging against their knees. We filled their plates with food, secure in our knowledge of their likes and dislikes. They cracked open the plastic eggs and spilled colorful treasure onto the grass, small miracles released from sweaty hands. Soon these trinkets would wind up lost in plastic toy buckets in our homes. They would litter the bottoms of drawers or sit unclaimed on top of clothes dryers, steadily losing their shine. But for now, there was nothing more cherished than a small whelk, pink at the fluted mouth, or a shard of polished blue glass.

Distracted by this plenty, no one looked up when a young man arrived. But our friend, the hostess, noticed and welcomed him. She touched his sleeve and announced that he was a Ukrainian student sponsored by her husband's firm. The rest of us looked up briefly from our plates and our children to the man with the ponytail and uncared-for goatee, whose skin shone through the fine weave of his white linen shirt. We took it in that he was not a parent or a child, but a foreigner here for the academic year. No one quite caught his name, but one of us handed him an empty plate and pointed him toward the buffet. He helped himself and took a seat on the patio beside the potted palm.

It was when the hostess set down lunch before her young son at the children's table that we first heard mention of the bird. We saw an inkling of concern cross her face as one of the older boys pressed her son.

"Come on," he asked, "you didn't keep it, did you?"

The hostess exchanged a look with us, then crouched beside her boy and began to ask questions. Shocked by his reply, the newest mother among us veered off and told her husband, which struck us as wholly unnecessary. But it was too late and the men swooped in. Our hostess—the very reason for us being there on this fine Easter morning—was elbowed to the side as the boy's father took over. It was out of our hands now.

"You had better show me," the boy's father said quite sternly.

So the little boy left his plate on the table and tromped upstairs to his bedroom under the eaves with his father and several of the men following. We would soon join them, but first we watched as the mother called across the patio to the Ukrainian student. We suspected she had something in mind, and although she stumbled publicly over his unusual name, the student nodded politely, set down his food, and made his way through the kitchen and up to the boy's bedroom, too.

The son stood blocking his little bedside table as he said to his father, "It's OK, Dad. Really, it is."

The father knelt down, all severity gone from his voice. "But, when something dies, it's dead."

We peered into the low-ceilinged room and watched the bent men, our husbands, as they gazed around helplessly, as if they'd never been in a boy's bedroom before. We recognized the singular, unsettled look in their eyes as they waited to see the bird.

"Excuse me," the foreign student asked as he stepped over the threshold, "what is problem?"

Not to worry, one of the men said, just a typical boyhood thing. A grackle had crashed into the kitchen window and died. The father and his young son had buried it in the backyard, but apparently the boy, being curious—being a boy, another father chimed in—had dug it up. No big deal, the men said and nodded in agreement.

"And where is bird now?" the Ukrainian student asked.

The boy stepped aside and glanced at the bottom drawer.

"Jesus," the father said, running a hand through his thinning hair, "in there with your toys and things?"

"I've been taking care of it," the boy said.

"How many days?" one of the men asked.

"It likes it here. Please don't take it away," the boy pleaded.

"Perhaps," the foreign student suggested, "we move small furniture outside?"

At that idea, two men lunged at the small table and carried it down the stairs. We followed behind the student as the procession of men wove back through the house and outside again.

"I don't know what to tell you, son," the father said and took the boy's small hand. "When something dies, its soul goes up to heaven, but its body stays here and gets pretty gross. It's not something you want to see."

"I wanted to see," the boy said.

And although we didn't like gross things, we could understand the boy's point of view. You did want to see. Sometimes you did.

Out on the driveway, the men set down the bedside table and the foreign student returned to his plate of food on the patio. The husbands we knew so well stood around the dresser and one of them picked at the Superman sticker on top. It amused us to see them so flummoxed. They shuffled in place while the father talked with his son where the boy had squeezed himself between two trashcans in the driveway and was crying.

"I was taking care of it," he repeated.

"I know," the father said, "I'm sorry, buddy."

Which was the only answer worth giving, we thought. But the men were impatient, eager to open the drawer and see what was inside. They called for the father to hurry up. So he squeezed his son's shoulder and the boy ran off into the yard.

It was the father who opened the drawer and leaned down to look more closely. The smell of the bird hit everyone just then, but we edged nearer anyway, and saw the slick black bird lying on its side. Its neck was flung back as if in song, the body writhing with maggots. The few of us who pressed close turned away, but then turned back again and watched as the men studied the carcass that swarmed with white movement. They appeared unbothered by the way the worms moved in and out of the open eye that faced them. More crawled through the mouth and around the yellowish beak. One of the men explained that the heat of the sun was making the worms writhe more actively, as if he had known that before this very moment, as if he and the other men understood the most elemental nature of things.

We peered around them and noticed the way the worms curled past the plastic action figures and the marbles and the shiny little bell left in the corner of the drawer. We knew with great certainty that the mother had given the boy those things the previous Easter and this moment illustrated the fate of so much. All our efforts, the packages wrapped with ribbon and fine paper, the gifts bought and bestowed, in time came to resemble this drawer—entangled and slimy and just plain ruined. Not a cheerful thought for an Easter morning, but there it was for all the world to see, writhing in the sun.

The men said nothing and we said nothing. But when they had satisfied their curiosity, they pulled away, stepped back, and surveyed the yard, as if they were members of a mountain expedition arrived at the summit, while we and the bird remained far below at base camp.

Seeing such somber faces, our friend, the hostess, left behind the rest of the guests who continued to eat and drink and chat with one another on the patio. She rushed over and tried not to gag when she looked down into the open drawer.

"Oh, God," she said.

We worried briefly that she wouldn't know what to do next, but of course she did. That was how it was: the men claimed the top of the mountain, while the women tilled the soiled below. But before she offered a solution, our friend and hostess gazed across at the patio where she had seen to it that the others were having such a good time. The distance from the party still in progress to the dark shape writhing with maggots was hard to fathom. It seemed that now there was only the bird—beautiful and fascinating and dead. But that wasn't true. She would see to it that the party carried on.

Our hostess then called out to the Ukrainian student for the second time that day. He set down his plate again and walked around the children who were sprawled on the patio eating their chocolate eggs. The young man glanced down without expression at the bird.

"Yes, madam?" he asked.

"We know you're one of the University Fellows, but what precisely is it that you study?"

"I am exchange divinity student."

"How perfect," the wife said, her face flushed. We assumed the champagne punch was getting to her, as it was to us, which only gave us more faith in her. "And what divinity is it that you divine?" she asked.

"The Orthodox Church, of course."

"Fine, fine, excellent. So, I assume you won't mind helping us at this difficult moment." She glanced back at the bird, and her hand, as if of its own volition, reached gently to pat the student's elbow through his gauzy shirt. She then told him what to do.

The men nodded as if they had been thinking of it themselves. But then they stepped away deferentially and appeared grateful to find their beers and plates where they had left them.

A short while later and with a certain satisfaction and a sense of inevitability, we brought our husbands along with us as we tromped to the back of the yard, following in the wake of our friend. Her husband was already there, a shovel in hand and a hole dug in the soil at his feet. At first we did not see their son, but then we spotted him high up in a nearby maple tree. He looked down from what we assumed was his favorite limb as the other children gathered around the foreign student. The young man in the white shirt and long ponytail lifted the bird into his hands and held it aloft for a long moment before setting it down into the hole. The feathered corpse slid from his fingers, the stiff body flopping over and revealing the hollow eyes.

The father used the shovel to quickly cover the bird with dirt, but the children had seen the eyes alive with worms. The littlest boys let out squeals of excitement as actual shivers overtook their bodies. The older boys growled, the word "awesome" ricocheting between them. The girls mostly feigned tears, or perhaps they truly did start to cry, which we could understand. Several girls pressed themselves against our skirts and we stroked their thin, warm hair.

The student then raised his hand over the grave and made the sign of the cross. Everyone listened carefully as he spoke in an ancient language none of us recognized. It made the younger children giggle and the older ones squeeze up their faces as if they just might understand. The parents—mothers and fathers alike—stood on the lawn, united in our hopes that we, too, could grasp not only the meaning of the words but of the dead bird as it found its home again beneath the earth on an Easter morning.

When the Ukrainian student finished speaking, we started to move away and left him alone beside the grave. He tamped it down with his shoe as the father returned the shovel to the tool shed. The other fathers strode across the lawn, but a few of us mothers stayed at the back of the yard. We looked down on the grave and the soil, black and churned up and damp.

Some of us wondered if our friend's son would try to dig the bird up again. If he did, we couldn't blame him, although by now he must have understood that the bird was finally, fully dead. Deader than before, when it had lain in the boy's drawer, one of us said, which made no sense, but somehow did. Now that it was buried, the boy could forget it more easily, one of us offered. Wasn't that the idea, we all wondered, to forget it once it was gone?

Although, we mothers could also imagine that the boy up in the tree was at that very moment swearing to himself that he would never forget the black bird that had been taken away from him and buried again on Easter Sunday. We had made such promises to ourselves when we were young, too. As our husbands sauntered away, carefree on the lawn, we had to ask ourselves how it was that we, more than our men, could relate to the poor, misunderstood boy. How was it that we still insisted to ourselves that we would never let a single thing pass us by, while our husbands seemed content with quite the opposite?

But then we noticed the father. He had circled back around and stood beneath the tree with his head tipped up. He spoke in hushed tones to his son. We couldn't catch the words, but just hearing the sounds made us wonder if, in fact, there was still hope for us all. Perhaps we weren't the only ones who understood there was nothing more important than a boy's unwillingness to let go of a bird.

From across the lawn came the cries of the little girls as they began to wail about the departed creature. The boys pelted them with tin foil from their chocolate eggs and chased them back onto the patio and around the garden. They wriggled their fingers in the air, pretending they were the maggots and the girls the dead bird. But they couldn't catch them. The girls were too fast. They ran ahead, flapping their wings, just out of reach.

Redbone

As he swam out from the shore, Tom Redbone thought
of many things—self-immolation and artistry, his
girlfriend Patty left sitting on the sand, the terrible
distraction of children that had almost done him in, his
wife's most recent nagging phone call, the long wait of
his career and now, finally, success. He had been up all
night. His arms ached with each stroke, yet he liked the
burning in his muscles, a minimal sacrifice to know he
was alive, very much alive. He had been so lucky, though
of course he had worked for it. God knew, he had worked.

The night before, a group had gathered on the shore
to watch him burn one of his paintings in a ritual he had
long considered, but which now seemed more potent
because the paintings were worth so much more. He had
meant for it to be a private thing, but with the arrival of
the curator, his dealer, and others documenting the
evening, Redbone had had no choice but to embrace the
fame. He was now in the public eye, his every gesture
captured and potentially added to an oeuvre known as
Redbone.

And he hadn't even needed to light himself on fire.
For months he had planned to self-immolate and dive

off the highest rock into the waves. It could be done and he would have done it. In the end, the gesture seemed gratuitous. Too 9/11: the reference bald, straightforward, lacking in subtlety. True, paintings had been burned before, but that was part of the point—a generic gesture meant to reference sacrifice in all cultures. Besides, he had never felt completely comfortable with the idea of singeing his skin. No, the flaming painting was sacrifice enough, especially since they were now fetching six figures.

His guests had stayed past three. Skeptical at first, eventually they got into the ritual and it worked the way he had hoped. The crowd felt a giddy sense of togetherness, a drunken connection to each other and a belief they were a part of something larger than themselves —something beyond that moment in time, beyond even the New York art scene. Who knew, the event might someday be a footnote in the annals of art history. *Redbone's First Sacrifice. Redbone's Action. Redbone's Happening.* He wondered if the morning *Times* would mention it.

But he was getting ahead of himself. All he'd ever hoped for was to have his work be part of a dialogue. As he framed that familiar thought, he couldn't help hearing how he would phrase it for the press: "*All I ever wanted was to be a part of a dialogue, a participant in the scene and to be seen.*" He cringed at the pompous voice echoing in his head. Redbone screamed into the water, "Dumb fuck," and listened as the ocean absorbed the sound.

Redbone's left leg throbbed slightly and he worried about the small blood clot lodged on that side of his groin. The doctors had given him the go ahead for his usual activities. No big deal. Though wouldn't it be poignant, no, ironic, no, actually downright tragic, for him to die of a blood clot in Long Island Sound on the morning after his now famous ritual and just after the Whitney—always moderately encouraging since his first Biennial ten years earlier—had finally offered him a one man show of his *Gillian* series? No question then that both the ritual the night before and his untimely demise would make the papers. Such poor timing, everyone would say.

Redbone stretched his arms forward and pulled. He needed to stay fit. Take care of himself. He had a future to protect now. Before, he could have tossed his life away and virtually had—just get Gillian going on the disposable years of Redbone's past. Now, he owed it to himself, to art, to posterity. He knew he'd better get back before Patty grew bored and headed into the city without him. She was hard to satisfy, a bit out of his league, and perhaps more trouble than she was worth. Every artist had his cross to bear for his muse or hoped-for muse. Gillian had been his first and only, so far. Patty, despite his pleadings, had never wanted the job. Anyway, who needed a reluctant muse when he had the most important show of his career to prepare for? What Redbone needed was to return to shore and get down to work.

Gillian skimmed the *Times*, ignoring the usual depressing headlines about troop build-up and the latest political fiascos at home. She flipped to the Arts section, hoping for relief. The air conditioning hadn't worked all weekend and the super was still out of town. She wiped a pale, languid hand across her brow, the same hand that her soon-to-be ex-husband had painted so many times. *Gillian's Hands. Gillian's Feet. Gillian's Breasts I*, first alone, and then later, *Gillian's Breasts II*, breastfeeding. As if she could be divided into neat parts like that, resembling high-tech accessories at a mega-store, each in their own tight packaging. The glossy surfaces of Redbone's paintings were as impenetrable as clamshell plastic, the kind that required sharp scissors or a box cutter to get through. She gazed at the full-page movie ads. What she needed was a decent flick later when the girls were at school. Two hours in excessive air conditioning and a handsome lead could do her wonders. Escape had never seemed as essential as now.

Gillian homed in on the "Arts, Briefly" column on the section's second page. She read the latest Metropolitan Opera gossip, shook her head at the young celebrity caught drunk driving over Labor Day, felt bored by the staggering amounts grossed by the latest blockbuster upon its surprising end-of-summer release. Then her eye shot to the indistinct photo of her almost-ex at what looked like a Boy Scout jamboree, a bonfire blazing behind him. Gillian let out a groan, at first softly and then louder, until her voice crackled the way the fire must have the night before. Her hands were shaking and she crumpled the edges of the paper. So that's why he had needed their beach house over the weekend.

"Irresponsible charlatan," she hissed. She and the girls had sweltered in the empty city for three long days so he could pull this stunt. Gillian threw the newspaper onto the breakfast dishes.

Across the table, Emma looked up from her book and frowned. She knew better than to ask.

"Your father!" Gillian said.

Emma picked up the section gingerly and squinted into the grainy photo. A large smile spread across her face and she called to her little sister. "Isabel. Come quick. Daddy's in the newspaper!"

Gillian stood and her chair fell to the linoleum. She didn't pick it up. "And on the first day of school. What impeccable timing. He always upstages us, doesn't he, girls? I bet he doesn't even realize it."

Her daughters weren't listening.

"I call that I get to cut it out and take it to school with me," Emma said.

"That's not fair," Isabel whined. "Just because Emma saw Daddy first."

"I get to, don't I, Mom? Isabel can take it tomorrow."

Gillian stood with her back to her daughters, staring at the middle distance, which wasn't far in their cramped Chelsea apartment. Isabel took an edge of the thin newspaper between her sweaty fingers and pulled. The page ripped down the center of their father's handsome, startled face.

Patty whispered into her cell phone. "He used to be a fuckup and that was endearing. But now that he's got his shit together, it's all so expected. I mean, you should have seen this thing last night. I can't believe they stayed. I know I saw them rolling their eyes and I don't mean in ecstasy. They were laughing at him. How could you not?"

"But you're not going to just leave him out there, are you?"

Patty sighed and rubbed a hand over the sand. "I wish I could. He's hidden the car keys somewhere in that dreadful house."

"You're terrible."

"He's terrible!"

"Still, the Whitney, that's some news."

"I know, it's impressive. So why am I not impressed? He's already passé. The others know it. They just aren't admitting it yet."

"Well, you be nice and he'll bring you home and you can let him slip away. That's what I do. I let them slip away."

Patty cupped moist grains in the curve of her palm. "All these months, I didn't mind him. But now he seems so, I don't know—sincere."

"The review of his last gallery show called him earnest."

"Yes, earnest, exactly!"

"Just get back to the city and you'll forget all about him."

Patty looked out at the distant black speck that was Redbone swimming farther and farther from shore. As she stood and headed up to the house, she decided she was forgetting him already.

Emma kept her hand on the two strips of newspaper taped together in her pocket. She had hit her sister hard with her fist and her mother had said, "Emma, I'll make you go back on the meds if you do that again." Her mother was the one who needed meds. She had tried some, Emma knew, but apparently not the right ones. Just before leaving, Emma had handed Isabel an ice cube for the pink spot on her arm. They hadn't said anything and Emma knew that Isabel needed to keep sobbing quietly so her mother would linger by her side. But they had exchanged a look, the two sisters, and it helped. Sometimes Emma thought Isabel was all she had.

Now she flattened the scrap of newspaper against her leg inside her front pocket. Her father was famous, she told herself. Everything would be all right; he had finally gotten what he wanted. He was going to have a show at the Whitney. Even her dumb friends knew about the Whitney. Her father had left them to do his work and now he had done it so he could come home. She hoped for this with all her heart, but she also suspected it wouldn't come true. She had watched *Parent Trap* a dozen times and loved it when the two sisters finally had both parents back under the same roof. She knew it was Hollywood, knew all about Lindsay Lohan's real life these days. But still, she could dream.

Emma boarded a city bus and took a seat next to an elderly lady who looked like a walrus. She had fur on her chin, dopey eyes and a wide, puffy tush that flopped over the edges of her seat. Emma remembered standing in front of the walrus and seals at the Central Park Zoo with her father. It had been a cold day and he had bought them hot chocolates that steamed up her glasses and burned Isabel's tongue. Her sister was always whining about something, but she settled down when they stepped into the Seal House and the startling gray creatures spun through water right there before them, so close you could reach out and practically touch them. Visiting from another zoo was a special walrus. A rare walrus, the sign had said that their father read aloud, although Emma could have just as easily read it to herself and told him so. Her father smiled at her anyway, not getting the hint, and tried to take her hand as he explained that the walrus had once been almost extinct.

"Doesn't it look like it's from another time?" he asked. "Prehistoric or something?"

Emma had squinted at the weird animal and tried to see what he meant. To her it looked like all the other strange, large animals in the world. Who was to say that a hippo or a rhino or a giraffe weren't from another time? Who was to say they themselves weren't, wrapped up in their snow parkas and fuzzy hats and shiny, pink boots? She wanted to tell this thought to her father. He, of all people, might understand. But Isabel was agreeing wildly with everything he read to her and taking his other hand, so Emma did, too, though without smiling or offering any encouragement. Their mother was angry with their father for a thousand and one reasons, few of which Emma fully understood. On principle, though, she tried not to smile in his direction. Still, there were those thoughts—surprising, odd ones only her father might understand, if she ever bothered to tell him.

"It's remarkable how certain animals survive while others go extinct," he said. "And always for the most complicated of reasons."

"What's extinct?" Isabel asked.

Emma would have bet anything her sister knew what it meant, but wanted him to stare at her kindly and part her bangs and answer in a soft voice.

Before their father had a chance to reply, Emma blurted out, "You're going extinct, aren't you, Daddy?"

Her father looked at her for a long moment and sucked in air. "I, I—"

"I bet you are. Pretty soon we're not going to see you at all."

"Oh, no, that's absolutely not true. Has your mother been saying that? Emma, you have to believe I'll always—"

Isabel, who had been listening with wide eyes when Emma said they wouldn't see their father anymore, burst into a howl. "Daddy," she said, clawing at his parka with long scratches, "Don't go."

As her father comforted Isabel, Emma turned back to the walrus. It deserved to be extinct, with that stupid mustache and pudgy nose that was just asking to be punched. Seated on the bus, Emma accidentally kicked the walrus lady's ankle beside her.

"Careful, dear," the woman said.

Emma flounced her shoulders away and pressed her nose to the window. In her pocket she tore at the newspaper clipping with her bitten-down fingernails. Little shreds disintegrated under her damp touch. She pulled it out, flattened it against the window and scrutinized the smudged photo. Her father, she decided, looked like a walrus, too, his face open and innocent and dumb.

The waves were higher than expected, so Redbone turned on his back and let the water lap over his chest. For fifty-two, he was still quite fit, usually able to swim close to an hour without fatigue. Salt stung the spot above his lip he had cut shaving. Redbone remembered when he was a

boy and had rested his chin on his hands against the edge
of the ceramic sink, watching his father shave. The smell
of the aftershave came back to him. Every morning, the
same smell—clean and optimistic.

His father took the train into the city, making a living
in corporate advertising. Sometime in high school,
Redbone had started wondering how his father could look
himself in the mirror, knowing he was a cog in the wheel
of commerce. But his father was a man of his time and
thought that a cog was a decent thing, a noble thing.
Redbone had never wanted anything to do with it.

And Gillian had agreed, until the girls were born and
New York became exorbitant. Then the time came for
him to buckle down. Only he hadn't. For an awfully long
time, he hadn't. She ended up hating him for it. He hated
himself, too, for the selfishness required, especially when
he'd left her and their daughters. But it had paid off, or
seemed, finally, to be paying off now.

Redbone turned onto his front again and let out a long
sigh. Then he dipped his head and started swimming
again in earnest. He began with a slow, easy breast stroke.
He could practically sleep while swimming, he knew the
movements so well. He had his father to thank for that.
Those many evenings at the neighborhood pool when
his old man had taught him the proper way to do it. His
father had cared about that—getting the arms to extend
fully, the legs to push all the way through. Had he ever
thanked his old man? Redbone wondered. He suspected
not. He wished his father could see his show at the
Whitney. Though he rarely thought of him, Redbone
wondered what his father would think of his son's success.

With the next smooth kick, Redbone's left leg
suddenly cramped. A shocking, searing pain shot from
his groin down to his knee. At first he thought he had
been bitten and searched the water around him, craning

his neck above the waves. No one had mentioned sharks this summer, but you never knew and wouldn't that be an altogether more violent event? There was no sign of a creature, no blood. The pain quickly subsided and he let himself use the leg again.

The next kick caused another sharp pain. He let the left leg dangle and treaded water, wondering what to do next. Redbone looked back toward the beach, trying to get his bearings. He had swum perhaps a half mile straight out from the coast. No one was out early on a foggy morning like this one. He looked for the spot he had set out from. Patty must have gone back up to the house. Redbone turned in the water and began the slow, unsteady swim toward shore.

His left leg was throbbing now, but nothing more, so long as he didn't use it. Instead, he relied on the rest of his strong body to move him forward. It occurred to him he was hobbled, not truly crippled, and something about that reminded him of Gillian when she was pregnant. Both times as she neared her due dates and the sciatica down her legs had worsened to an unbearable state, she had been insistent that she wasn't a patient or a weakling just because she was carrying a child. She was fully herself and as strong as an ox—those were her words—but to watch her move, you'd have thought she was ancient and riddled with pain. Her body, anyone could plainly see, had become an altar of sacrifice to the next generation. Every part of her strained with both life and misery. That was what he had wanted to capture in his portraits of her—the contradictory elements of elation and degradation, success and failure, life and death.

In one of their fights she had shouted that he was a misogynist, tearing her apart and setting her down in pieces on his canvases. All he wanted was to show every part of a body at once vibrantly alive and yet succumbing.

She was the everyday, heroic embodiment of the survival of the species. How had she not understood that, when the critics had seen it right away? He supposed, though, as he stroked the water, that their troubles had less to do with her misunderstanding of his art than with the rest of it—the rent, the children, Patty.

As he thought of his daughters, Redbone kicked stronger and another stabbing pain caught him, shooting upward from his groin this time. It was enough to make him go under for a moment, the waves splashing over his lips. He swallowed without thinking and cold salt water scratched the back of his throat. His fingers felt suddenly numb, his toes, too. A shiver went down his body and he flipped onto his back so he could feel the pale sun through the fog. He tried to calm himself and breathe. Breathe. His daughters. He thought about his daughters as he used his arms to pull toward land.

He would call them as soon as he returned and make a plan to take them somewhere, to the movies or out for ice cream. What Redbone really wanted, he realized, as the pain flowed into his hips and ribs, was to read to them before bed like he used to. Tuck them in at night. Gillian's lawyer had arranged it so he would not have overnight privileges, not for a long time, if ever. All because of Patty.

He flipped back onto his belly and searched the shore again. He still couldn't see her and quietly realized that despite his desire to be loved by her, his longing to be accepted by her friends, and how crucial she had been to his career, she didn't seem to matter all that much to him. Redbone tried to erase her now altogether from his mind. He needed to think only of the positive, the essential. If he had learned anything over the past few years, it was that painful single-mindedness paid off. He tried to concentrate on remembering the name of the last book he had read to Emma, the one about a lady mouse at a carnival. That seemed like the right sort of thought to escort him in the direction of land.

Redbone's arms were cramping now, too, the cold taking them over. The difficulty was mostly on his left side, so he turned to do the side stroke with his right. The current was mild, but still it seemed to smash against him, pushing him back from his destination. By working his one good leg and keeping his neck raised, no more sea water went into his mouth. He tried to steady his breath, insist on his breath, and it worked.

He was good at being insistent. He had gotten his way in so many things. Gillian had never wanted children, but he had. Then the girls had become Gillian's life, her art taking a backseat, and he had his work to do. He had pressed for a new studio and more time. Time was his biggest success. He had robbed others of it, mostly Gillian and the girls, stolen it from them to use for himself. His dealer had helped, building up his work, pushing for him, cajoling collectors and the Whitney curators to take him seriously. Redbone had had to do the same, taking himself more and more seriously. It was what a person did to succeed.

A pain shot up his left side and struck his chest. It fired all the way to his cheek and he involuntarily bit down on his tongue, letting out a howl, which the ocean water silenced as it slipped down his open throat. When *Artforum* had called him "earnest" it could have been the kiss of death. But the ball of his fame was already rolling and other reviewers had argued the point for him.

Redbone turned onto his back and tried to laugh it off, but no sound came. The waves were loud in his ears. He still loved the work. The work was everything, or almost everything. He was now merely a vehicle for the phenomenon known as *Tom Redbone*—artist of the moment. His entire left side was cramping. Also his right hand felt numb and his right leg was burning with overuse. He glanced toward shore, hoping for someone to see him. The gray of the land met the gray of the water as if it didn't matter where one stopped and the other began. Redbone noticed the line, so elegant from a distance as it separated the two disparate elements. That clean line was what it was all about.

He kicked hard with his better leg and paddled with his better arm. He considered shouting again, although no one was around to hear. Had he tried, his voice would have been drowned by the sound of the waves crashing on the beach. He stopped straining and listened. He had almost made it. Redbone thought he had never heard anything as hopeful as the sound of those waves stretching the final distance to shore.

He resumed his efforts although to little effect. He realized he was an idiot for having gone out so far on his own. What had he been thinking, so cavalier, as if he had many lives and not just one? Only a fool assumes so much. He was a father, for Christ's sake. Why hadn't he been able to understand that? Gillian was right and not right about him. He was a decent man like his father had been and yet he wasn't. Redbone panted for air, using only his right arm to keep himself afloat. He had assumed he would turn out like his old man in the end, not in terms of career, but somehow as a man. He had always meant to end up like that, solid and well loved. It occurred to him now that it might not happen.

The pain had risen up from his leg and rested like a heavy weight on his chest. His body felt stiff and cold and a metallic taste that could have been blood filled his mouth. He wondered if it was possible he had been made of metal all along. *Tom Redbone*—a sculpture of found iron like the ones he had made back in grad school. Only he was rusted now, his surfaces oxidized and rough, every part of him the color of dried blood, rigid and lifeless and as lonely as those pieces he had left behind on the gallery floor after his senior thesis show, knowing he could do better.

Redbone kicked as hard as he could but hardly moved. A thought came to him and he let himself accept that he still wanted his wife, the person he had spent an inordinate amount of time hating. Gillian would know how to breathe into his mouth at this very moment. She would understand he was drowning. No one else could see it, but Gillian had seen it all along and it had made her angry and cruel, but she had been right.

He wouldn't want to bother the girls with his troubles. He had hurt them enough already. Let them keep playing, he thought. They should keep playing. And that one hopeful thought helped him pull harder with his good arm.

Redbone could sense he was at the place where the sea sucked down a final time before breaking. Below him hung the shelf where you could catch the waves and ride them in. He had instructed Emma and Isabel that from the shore to this line was the Safety Zone. They were never allowed to swim beyond it. Redbone was amazed to realize he had made it to the Safety Zone, yet he could not get his legs under him to stand. If he could only make his legs do what he wanted, the water would come up only to his waist. But his body would not respond. Redbone opened his mouth to yell and a wave took away the sound.

He was all pain now, left and right sides, arms and legs, hands and feet, disconnected from each other and unable to function in any useful way. He was tied together only by pain. He could see now why Gillian had disliked the idea. A body, a person, was more than its disparate, desperate hurting parts. A life was more than its struggles. He was more than some primitive sacrifice, a cog in the wheel of life, a participant in a dialogue with death, a body tossed onto the fire of time.

Redbone's thoughts swirled around him. His artwork, his plans, all those crucial notions he had relied upon to convince himself and others that he was worth something—all of it washed over him like the sea wrack floating past his lips. His life was becoming a loose, incoherent mass of plankton swirling around his body. With all his strength, he tried to push the wisps from his face. His arms did not respond and the seaweed slipped along his neck and clung to his heaving chest.

Redbone's only hope was that the waves might be kind and push him up onto the sand. As water filled his ears, he tried listening for the patient sucking in and the pulling back out of the breaking ocean. He thought that the waves gently crashing were speaking to him, saying, *Shush, shush,* as if trying to silence his worries. They were the sweet words spoken to a troubled child before sleep. The gently crashing waves were tucking him in.

As he became lulled by the bedtime story of the sea, Redbone let the water flow in and out of his gaping mouth. His throat convulsed in a cough, which took the last of his strength. The waves sounded stronger now and more harsh—*sorry,* they seemed to be saying, *so sorry.*

Redbone wanted to understand. He tried coughing the water from his throat, but could not. Were the waves singing to him a long, endless apology? Or was the song one of his own making, the one he had stubbornly pushed to the back of his mind and tried to ignore although it had played softly, continuously, for years? He heard the song he had meant to sing to his father and his daughters and Gillian—the woman, not the artwork. He recognized in the sibilant sounds the ache of his own shame.

Her Mother's Garden

In that first autumn after college, Annie rented an apartment in Cambridge and began to spend her evenings roaming the bookstores of Harvard Square. She found herself looking not so much for someone or something, but for a life she sensed was just out there waiting for her to discover it. If she saw a man who intrigued her, she would sometimes catch herself imagining them together in older age, reading in parallel chairs on a porch at dusk overlooking a garden they had tended that day. But that was her parents' fantasy—her parents' life—and Annie chided herself for the narrowness of her vision.

She had an entry-level publishing position in Boston that promised no particular future but made her feel as if she were striking out on her own. As fall gave way to winter and spring and then summer, she spent more and more time at her parents' house on the hill in a suburb west of Cambridge. She would kneel beside her mother as they planted dahlia bulbs in the back border of the garden. They wandered down the paths that wove past the fish pool and the ferns, past the hammock and the bee balm in full bloom, past the Rose of Sharon with blossoms a tearful blue as shadows stretched deep in late afternoon. In August, the green of the lawn rose up to meet them.

A year after she'd moved to Cambridge, Annie quit her publishing job without another one lined up. Harebrained, her father said, foolish. Her mother asked her out to the house that weekend to gather fallen crab apples and to help them rake. Annie and her parents piled leaves onto tarps, which they carried to the compost heap by the old stone wall. Her father's back was bad now and her mother's knees hurt each time she bent, so they quit early, but Annie kept working in the yard.

She raked past dusk and even weeded a bit as well, though her mother had not asked her to. When she walked back up the lawn after putting away her tools in the shed, she studied her parents as they sat on the flagstone patio looking out at the garden they had made. They weren't talking, but shared the same contented expression as they surveyed the yard.

Over the next several years, Annie went from job to job. She sold women's clothing at a shop in Harvard Square, did part-time secretarial work at a law firm, and then became an assistant to an assistant dean at the university. Finally, a friend left her position as a librarian at a private middle school and Annie took her place. She finished at three every afternoon, jogged beside the Charles River, met friends for coffee, read, and more and more often, visited her parents. They were getting elderly and not going out as much. The yard was a lot of work, her mother said, and while she never asked outright for help, Annie took it for the plea that it was.

On weekends, she went out to the house and worked all day in the yard, doing what her mother had done all those years. Now her mother no longer had to tell her which tasks to do or how to do them. Annie knew. It was still her mother's garden, but somehow it was Annie's as well. When she returned to work on Mondays she felt a strange satisfaction. She knew she should be more ambitious in life, develop a career, but when she stopped to think about it, she wondered if she had ever been happier than when working in her mother's garden, wiping stray hair off her forehead with the back of her arm, and taking in the quiet beauty of the place.

One afternoon, as she prepared to close up the library at the end of the school day, a father came in with a child's book in hand. Annie always cordially accepted library books brought in by parents, but would encourage them to have their children return the book themselves the next time. The man looked familiar, and as she prepared to offer her usual polite scolding, he said, "Annie? Annie James?"

She nodded, put off by the almost-laugh in his voice, as if he thought her name was amusing. But then she recognized him. "Freddie Marcatelli?" she asked.

He smiled modestly and looked down at his loafers. His head of dark hair caught the overhead lights. She tried to remember if his face had always been so sleek and if, as a teenager, his skin had had that ruddy glow. A forgotten wealth of thoughts about this man returned to her. Although she hadn't considered his existence for more than fifteen years, she suddenly remembered that in high school Freddie had been the captain of both the football and the ice hockey teams. He had shoulders so broad the girls used to joke that he wore football pads to class under his shirts.

Annie recalled now that he had surprised everyone at the end of senior year by reaching outside his usual circle of jocks and cheerleaders to invite Annie's best friend to the prom. A confident, artsy girl who grew up a few houses away from Annie, Caitlin Carmichael had actually turned Freddie down, a decision that went against the natural order of things at their high school and shocked everyone. Instead, Freddie ended up taking a glamorous, buxom, blond townie, who some people said was one of his cousins.

Most of the girls in their class would have died to go out with Freddie Marcatelli. Annie had wondered at the time if she would have agreed to go with him, not that she thought he had ever really noticed her. Caitlin and their friends made fun of him behind his back, calling him a gorilla and a thug, but Annie had secretly thought him disturbingly appealing. Freddie had the kind of toughness that no one she knew possessed. His father had been the town's police captain and several of his uncles were firemen. Dozens of Marcatellis populated the public schools and the neighborhoods near the center of town, but none lived on the hill where Annie had been raised among academics like her father, as well as surgeons, lawyers, and even a judge or two.

But now, as Freddie's flecked brown eyes twinkled and he offered a cocky half smile, she recalled how he had also surprised everyone by getting into Harvard. Maybe not such a dumbshit after all, everyone whispered. Apparently, he'd been among the first in his family to go to more than a community college and certainly the first accepted at Harvard.

"Thanks for bringing it back," she said, relieved to look away from him and instead at the book she accepted from his hand. "We try to get the kids to take responsibility for the ones they check out."

"No problem, next time Mattie will return it himself. The kid's a knucklehead. Just like I was, right?"

Annie laughed and found herself defending the boy. "I know Matt. He's a good boy."

Freddie shook his head and kept smiling at her. "Wow, Annie James. You used to wear those cute little ribbons in your hair that matched your outfits."

"No, I didn't."

"Sure you did. On the bus in elementary school."

She had forgotten that she and Freddie had been in elementary school together, too.

"The bus picked you kids up on the hill last. I never could get you and Caitlin to notice me. I was just another townie in the back of the bus. You probably thought I was a real fuck-up."

Annie looked around at the hushed library and dropped her voice, "You weren't a fuck-up. You did great in high school. *You* went to Harvard."

"Yeah, I still think my old man pulled a few strings on that one."

Annie let out a disbelieving puff of air. Her father, Harvard alum and distinguished professor, had not been able to do the same for her. If Freddie had gotten in, it was because he belonged there.

"Long story," he said.

Freddie, who went by Fred now, offered to tell her about it over a cup of coffee. That Saturday morning after he dropped his son off at soccer practice down at the field by the high school, he zipped into Cambridge in his convertible and picked her up, then drove them back out to the bagel place in the suburban town where they had been raised. It turned out he still lived there in the same neighborhood as his cousins and parents. He'd gotten married to a fellow dermatologist, but it hadn't worked out. She was too independent, not family-minded enough for him. Fred beat her out in court and won the boy. Those were his words: *beat her out and won the boy.*

As he explained how he worked his dermatology practice around little Mattie's after-school sports schedule, Annie fidgeted with the sugar packets on the table. Decent kid, Fred said, little hellion, like he'd been: the boy needed a firm hand to keep him in line. Annie trembled imperceptibly as she worried for Fred's son. Yet, she also felt strangely jealous of him, too. It would be something to have Fred Marcatelli on one's side in life.

He leaned across the table. "You haven't changed a bit. Still so quiet. Come on, speak up, Annie James. Tell the whole world about you."

"Really," she said, "there isn't much to say."

Soon they began seeing each other on Saturday afternoons that then rolled into Saturday evenings. He took her to his favorite Italian place in the South End, followed by the Boston Symphony. To her surprise, he had season tickets to the concerts as well as to the Bruins in Boston Garden. He often arrived with something in hand—special flowers for her, and not just the kind from the grocery store, or a book of poetry he'd heard Garrison Keillor read from on the radio. Fred brought skeins of hand-dyed yarn and goat cheese made by local farmers, things he thought might appeal to her, but which he himself admitted to knowing little about.

In her less charitable moments, Annie thought that he was using her to imagine a more refined life for himself. He was finally capturing one of the bright girls from the hill who came from bookish homes and carried a Cambridge pedigree, something perhaps he prized over money or good looks. But anyone could see that Fred was the more attractive of the two, and clearly more successful. The truth was, Annie didn't know why he was dating her. She supposed that mystery kept her involved.

He was polite and gracious, better mannered than the men she had gone with in college. He called her in the morning to ask if she had enjoyed herself the evening before. He called at five o'clock in the afternoon to ask how her day at work had gone. No pressure, he said, no rush, which made Annie wonder what it was they weren't rushing toward.

"Annie, Annie James," Fred said at Giacomo's, where the maître d' had whisked them past lines of tourists and seated them at Fred's usual table, "there's more to you than meets the eye. You cool girls were always so secretive. Tell me a secret, Annie."

While she appreciated his high hopes about her and felt it must be true that she had secrets tucked close to her heart, she wasn't entirely sure if Fred Marcatelli was the one to know them. The two boys she had gone out with during college—they had never called it dating exactly—had seemed so much more elusive, self-involved, overly smart and yet, she somehow knew them better. They were men in the mold of her father. Men with ambitions first and the women after: men whom her mother had warned her about and yet assumed she would marry. But with Fred, she was his interest; she—or who he thought she was—was his ambition. Annie couldn't decide if she liked that or not.

The following spring, after they had been dating for some months, Annie decided it was time for him to meet her parents. To hide him any longer from them didn't seem right and a visit to the house could serve as a litmus test of her seriousness about the relationship. The truth was, she needed her mother's perspective.

One dusky evening in early June when the sky parted after several days of rain and the sun had become unseasonably warm, Annie walked with Fred down the side path to the backyard. She didn't hold his hand, but could sense his eager steps behind her on the flagstones. He pressed his fingers into her shoulder as if steering her, and Annie couldn't tell if she was about to introduce him to her mother's garden, or if she was being marched there against her will by him instead.

"Heavens," her mother said when Fred firmly shook her hand, "of course I remember you. You were a big bruiser of a fellow."

Fred smiled and took this as a compliment.

Annie's father couldn't get out of bed for supper. He'd been ill off and on all spring, and the night before had been bad.

"I'll make us all a simple dinner," Annie said. "Soup or something from the cabinets. We can take it up to Dad on a tray."

"No, come on, let's do take out," Fred said. "It's on me. The Parthenon makes fantastic chicken and rice soup. Old Greek recipe and excellent for your health. I bet Mr. James will like it."

As Annie had the urge to remind him to call her father "Professor," Annie's mother chimed in, "I suspect he will. Thank you, Fred. That's a lovely idea."

Fred wrapped a big arm around Annie's mother's shoulder and squeezed her to his side. "That'a girl, Mrs. J.," he said, which only made Annie's mother smile more. As he placed the order from his cell phone, Annie tried to tell if her mother was being sincere. Didn't it bother her that Fred patronized her in that way? It worried Annie that her mother was so preoccupied with her father's health that she could no longer be relied upon for a second opinion about this man who had placed himself at the center of Annie's life.

"Why don't you give him the grand tour of the garden, Annie? Show him everything," her mother said.

In the backyard, Fred held onto Annie as if he couldn't get enough of her, his hands on her waist, on her arms, his fingers laced tightly in hers. He must have seen the pride on her face as she pointed out the beauty of the garden and he tried to reflect it back to her.

"So this is it," he said, "This is where my girl grew up."

She strolled past the ferns, the hammock, and the mammoth oak. She pointed at the koi in the fishpond and the way the hostas and vinca flowed so nicely around the rocks. She was about to take Fred down the sloping lawn past the laurels, when he pulled her to him and kissed her. Annie firmly pushed him away.

"What? What are you worried about?" he asked. "Your mother can't see us all the way down here. With those cataracts, she probably can't see past the whatever-you-call those pots up there on the patio."

"Geraniums," Annie said. "White geraniums."

"I knew that."

Annie turned and started back up the lawn.

"Wait," he called after her, "what are you mad about? That's true about her eyes, you know. Come on, show me the rest. Give me the grand tour, Annie James."

She hated the cocky tone of his voice, how it seemed almost mocking, but also laced with something resembling envy, even awe. Whatever it was, she hated that he probably did know a white geranium when he saw one; hated that she had brought him to her mother's garden in the first place. She had meant to keep it a secret. She had meant to save it for someone special.

As her steps landed too hard on the flagstone patio, it occurred to Annie that in recent years she had always come here alone. There hadn't been someone else, friend or lover, to share it with for some time now. She told herself she needed to give Fred a real chance. There were other men out there, of course, but it all took so much effort. She couldn't count on herself to do it all over again, the painful business of getting close to someone new. Knowing her, Annie thought, she'd stay holed up reading in her apartment, or puttering here in the backyard as the years slipped away. Fred was right here, right now, and more than decent. For whatever reason, he seemed to like her better than she could recall anyone liking her before.

On the patio, her mother greeted her with her same worrisome, overly bright smile. "He's awfully nice," she said.

Annie wanted her to say more, to tell her what to do. But her mother turned back inside. Annie looked across the lawn to where Fred Marcatelli surveyed the beds, his head bent over the spring phlox as if meeting a child for the first time.

At supper, Annie did her best to be civil to him. He pulled out a seat for her mother, served the spanakopita— apparently a favorite of her mother's, though Annie had never known it. She and Annie's father had had it in Greece years before Annie was born. She told them about an exotic outdoor restaurant perched on a hillside surrounded by olive trees and waiters who danced on the tables after supper. Annie hadn't heard her mother speak so animatedly in some time.

After their meal, Fred told the ladies to stay seated while he ducked into the kitchen and dished out overly large scoops of Annie's mother's favorite ice cream into the Waterford crystal dishes that she normally saved for special occasions. How Fred had thought to find the bowls in the back of the cabinet was a mystery.

"He certainly has style," Annie's mother whispered when he went back for spoons. And Annie had to agree.

All that winter, Annie debated in her mind the question of Fred Marcatelli. When Caitlin called from Los Angeles around Christmastime, Annie didn't tell her about him. She couldn't bear to hear the jokes that would ensue, especially knowing they would be good ones. She just hoped that Fred would somehow disappear and she'd never have to admit to having almost loved him.

For it wasn't out of the question that she could come to love Fred Marcatelli. Life was full of such strange twists as loving someone who you had ridden with on a school bus in second grade, someone you had alternately loathed and desired in high school. He was everything she wasn't, then and now, and perhaps that was as it should be. But

Annie hardly had time for such considerations. Her parents were dwindling, and their health and futures occupied more and more of her mind, even as they receded from view.

In January, her father had a fall. After two weeks in the hospital, he spent another three in a dreadful rehab center. Thanksgiving week, he finally came home. Annie's mother seemed exhausted and she hadn't even started to care for him yet. The house couldn't possibly work for a wheelchair. Visiting nurses needed to be contacted, safety bars put up in the bathrooms, a hospital bed in the living room. Annie couldn't see how her mother, not to mention she, would have the energy to cope with it all.

She spent that winter caring for her mother while the nurses cared for her father. On the weekends, she and her mother grocery shopped, made meals that her mother could defrost during the week, made lists of doctors Annie would contact during her lunch hours at the school. Her principal was understanding and let her off to take both parents to doctor appointments. Then, in April, doctors found a lump in her mother's breast.

Annie and her mother sat side by side that evening on the sofa and looked at garden catalogues. Annie's mother circled the bulbs and perennials she hoped to plant, although they both knew she would not order them. Spring came in a blanket of New England gray that suddenly opened into green. Weeds popped up along the pathways. The azaleas bloomed and soon needed to be trimmed and fertilized. Annie meant to plant impatiens around the fish pool as always, but couldn't seem to get to it. Her father needed the curtains drawn anyway because the sunlight hurt his eyes, so what did it matter? No one went into the garden much anymore.

One Saturday morning when Annie was packing an overnight bag and preparing to go out to her parents for the weekend, the doorbell of her apartment rang. Instead of buzzing in whoever was there—no doubt the mailman dropping off a package—she hurried down the stairs and flung open the door. There stood the great bulk of Fred Marcatelli with a small, white envelope in his hand.

Annie had tried to keep him abreast of her parents' situation through the previous months, but had hardly noticed when he stopped calling as often. As she looked up into his clean-shaven, handsome face, she felt as if she hadn't seen him for years, perhaps not since high school. He appeared fresh and undaunted, willing to pick up wherever they had left off. When Fred heard her weekend plans, he offered to give her a lift out to her parents' house. Annie usually took the bus so she was grateful for the offer.

She climbed into his convertible and her legs felt heavy and cumbersome. They set off and the slipstream did not disturb her hair, pulled back harshly into a ponytail. Unlike the car, nothing about her felt youthful or lithe. At the wheel, Fred looked terrific as usual, unperturbed by age. He had to shout above the sound of the wind as they drove out Memorial Drive.

"So sorry about your folks, Annie," he said. "But I got a little something for you and your mom this morning."

He dropped the envelope into Annie's lap and she picked it up between pale fingers.

"Don't open it. They'll fall out. It's some sort of seeds. A special type of morning glory," Fred said with a pleased smile that led effortlessly into a wink. "Very rare. The man at the nursery said it was a find."

Annie shook the envelope and heard the rattle of dry seeds. Annie thanked him and Fred seemed genuinely pleased. Pleased enough to put his hand on her knee. He was a good guy, she decided, decent-hearted and even kind. Annie understood that morning glories were as common as weeds, but Fred didn't know that. Perhaps the nurseryman had hoodwinked him. But still, the idea was sweet, and as he squeezed her knee they shared the pleasure of his good deed.

At the house, Annie didn't stop him from following her down the side path and around to the backyard. They stepped across the flagstone patio and she wondered if he noticed the way the weeds had weaseled their way between the cracks. Fred slid open the glass door that opened onto the dining room and a thick, sickly smell struck them both. The thermostat had been turned up so high the air felt like a pressure against Annie's dry eyes. Her mother asked them to close it fast. Fred did so, bowing a little as strapping men will when stepping too quickly into a room, their vigor too much for the place.

"Your father hates the light now," Annie's mother said with a sigh.

Annie hugged her mother and felt the bones of her spine. She kept a grip on her for too long before letting go.

Fred stayed with Annie that entire afternoon and helped around the house. There was so much to be done on the weekends when the nurse was off. At one point late in the day, they took a break and Annie let him rub her shoulders as she looked out the kitchen window at the garden. Tears appeared at the corners of her eyes as she stared out at the ancient oak, which her mother had been trying to keep alive with expensive treatments although it was diseased. Annie studied the vacant spot where the hammock was supposed to be. No one had even bothered to bring it out although it was June already. The trail leading down past the laurels had become overgrown. The shrubs were leggy and needed attention.

"It's all so much work," she said.

Fred took her hands and pulled her to sit at the kitchen

table opposite him. "Annie, I hate to break it to you, but they can't live here anymore," he said. "I mean, come on."

She nodded.

"There are places that take care of people at this stage. They need more help than you can possibly give them. Your mother can't handle all this."

It wasn't that Annie and her mother hadn't thought about this dilemma before. Annie had made the requisite calls. "The retirement places all have five-year waiting lists," she explained. "I don't know why we put it off for so long. I don't think we have options now."

"I know people," Fred said. "I can talk to people."

Annie looked at him and couldn't quite remember who he was or why he was here.

"Do you want me to talk to the people I know?" he asked.

Annie nodded again.

"Good." He slapped his hands on his thighs and stood. "I just hate to see this," he waved his hands at the room. "A beautiful place like this falling into disrepair."

Annie looked around, too. He was right. The house looked awful. The kitchen cabinets were old and soiled with decades of fingerprints. The counters had peeled up in places and were stained. The faucet was rusted. The refrigerator hummed so loudly you had to talk louder in its presence. Sometimes it sent a slow, sad trickle of dirty water across the linoleum. Why hadn't she noticed the decay before? Like her parents, was she aging alongside this home and remaining blind to its decrepitude and her own?

Fred put his hands on his hips and said, "You'll want to put the house on the market, I think."

Annie tried not to let him see her shock.

"This neighborhood up here on the hill, a good size parcel of land—you'll do all right. Might even make a decent deal. Someone will want to turn it around. Fix it up and sell it again. I've got a great broker for you. You want me to call my broker?"

At first, Annie didn't even know what he meant. A financial person, she wondered? She stared at him for a long moment and finally smiled weakly, not meaning to be rude. Her eyes burned from lack of sleep and the top of her head throbbed with a dizzying headache.

"She's a cousin of mine in real estate."

"Thank you, Fred. That sounds right."

July came. Glorious, blue-skied July, but Annie and her mother stayed stuck inside. They cleared out junk from the attic and basement, old woolens in the cabinets, shoeboxes of letters, shelves of stemware and china. As they worked side by side in the dusty corners of the house, they both wanted more than anything to be in the yard. Some late afternoons, Annie finally broke free and went out. The wild summer plants and weeds had taken over the pathways and beds. It was depressing not to get to them, but equally depressing once she did.

The groundhogs that her mother had fought for years in campaigns like a military general had chewed off the blooms of most of her perennials. The giant oak had lost its leaves into the fishpond, where they clogged the filter. Whole limbs hung bare. Annie now walked down past the laurels and noticed that the lawn, once so lush and inviting, had humps in long lines from moles. The laurels still had pink and white fairy skirts, but the blossoms seemed dwarfed and insignificant compared to the enormity of the chaos around them. There wasn't much Annie could do, not much at all, once nature had decided to take back the garden.

Finally in November, her parents were admitted to the retirement community that Fred had helped arrange. Annie had hardly slept for weeks. Her arms ached from carrying boxes and then from the emptiness the boxes left behind. Her mother hated the cramped apartment, the windows that wouldn't open come springtime, the tiny sun porch that overlooked a parking lot and, beyond it, an anonymous water tower in a town she didn't know.

Just three indoor plants, transplants from her garden, sat neglected on the coffee table. Annie tried to remember to water them each time she visited, but within weeks they had died. She unceremoniously threw them into the garbage chute without mentioning it to her mother. Annie tried to tell her mother that they were lucky the retirement home had worked out, but her mother's eyes were red all the time. The grief she felt for all she had lost was so great, Annie could hardly stand to look at her.

Meanwhile, her parents' house remained unsold. Months passed. Finally in spring, Babs, the broker, told her they were going to drop the price, do several open houses in a row, beef up their internet presence, but if none of that worked by August, they would be forced to sell it at auction. Babs was no-nonsense and did most of her business by cell phone. When she did appear, she had a clipboard held high in her sculpted arms. She was always on her way to or from the gym. Annie hadn't even taken a walk in months. She'd been so busy, overwhelmed. She told herself not to be intimidated by Babs, who was, after all, working for Annie and her parents.

It dogged Annie that Babs looked familiar. When she finally got around to asking how they might have known each other, Babs laughed and said, "All us Marcatellis look alike."

Now that she mentioned it, Annie recognized the aquiline nose and broad shoulders.

"Maybe you remember me from Freddie's prom. I was *that* girl," she said and rolled her eyes, as if it had all been a joke.

Annie had the strange sensation that her life was being recast with others in the leading roles. Her story was an inconsequential footnote in another family's much longer and more rewarding tale. This woman before her was the beauty who had stolen her school's best-looking guy. But to Babs, Fred was just family. And Annie, well, she was nobody.

August came and Babs appeared at Annie's apartment to make the case for selling the house at auction. Annie didn't understand why an old house in a respected neighborhood wouldn't attract buyers. She knew it was in disrepair, but couldn't people see past that? And besides, the garden was so lovely, even when not at its best.

"You just don't see grand old trees like those anymore," Annie said.

"People don't want old trees," Babs said. "You've got younger and younger buyers who want a clean slate. They want easy homes. Clean homes. Low maintenance homes. I have to warn you, whoever buys your place is likely to knock down the old trees, maybe even all of it."

"All of it?"

"The house, the yard, all of it."

"But why?"

"They want new. Not used, especially not used up. You know, worn out. I'm sorry, but that's how it is."

"But the trees?" Annie repeated.

"Trees fall on houses. Trees clog up gutters. Buyers want to protect their investment."

Annie nodded. She had never thought of her family home as an investment. She chided herself for being stupid about such an obvious thing. Perhaps if she'd ever owned her own home she might have understood. But it made her worry that in some fundamental way she didn't grasp how things really worked in life. She never had, and now it might be too late for her to change.

Finally, with Babs' persuasiveness, Annie agreed to the auction. They needed money to cover the cost of all those months of home nursing and now the retirement place.

Her father, though hardly able to speak anymore, had made it clear he wanted something to come down to Annie. He wished he could give her the house, but they had to cover their costs. He was concerned about her mother after he was gone. He wanted her to be well taken care of. Annie understood all this and agreed to the auction.

On the last weekend in August, she wandered through the empty rooms of her parents' home. She rubbed her toes over the stained floorboards and collected dust from the chipped windowsills. Without their furniture and things, it was just a house. Then she wandered outside.

The day was hot, muggy, and the overgrown garden was filled with silence. She stood looking out as she had on summer mornings when her mother worked amid the many plants and trees, propagating, tending—caring for it all. Annie wanted to call out to her, had wanted to call out to her for months, but her voice had stayed strangled in her throat. Sometime in late winter she had stopped crying, and now she wished she could recover all those unshed tears and release them.

As Annie headed off the patio and wandered down the rocky path in the direction of the little choked pond, she heard a car pull into the driveway. She turned to see Fred Marcatelli's convertible ease toward her and park on the cracked asphalt under the oak's bare limbs. He climbed out and strode forward.

"Annie," he called. "I figured I'd find you here."

She let him hug her and kiss her lightly on the lips.

He glanced at the yard, then said, "Hey, listen, I've got an idea."

Annie vaguely wondered if he saw the changes all around them. Did he notice what time had done to this place, to her and to her family? Then she reminded herself that of course he did. He had been the one who had seen it coming even before she had.

"I've come to a decision," he said.

She stared into his open, confident face, amazed that such an uncluttered mind could exist anymore.

"I want to buy your folks' house."

Annie let go of his hand, but he grabbed it back again.

"Now, hear me out. If it goes to auction, Babs says that they're going to get only half, if you're lucky two-thirds, of what your folks originally asked. That's a lot of change to lose. The market just sucks these days. I can offer three quarters of the original asking price. That's more than fair, Annie. The place is a pit now, pardon the expression. But it could be worth it for me, for us both. What do you say?"

Annie slipped away from him and wandered over to the old oak. She leaned her back against it and the ridges poked her harshly between the shoulder blades. She pressed into them and tried to steady herself.

"You have that kind of money?" she asked.

He laughed.

The mystery of Freddie Marcatelli, of all the Freddie Marcatellis of the world, spread open before her. There were families like hers, Annie realized, families that aged and died out. Decent families that somehow didn't seize the day. And then there were families like the Marcatellis, with Babs and Fred and all the cousins, and the parents down in Florida half the year, on the Cape for the other half. Families who thrived and lasted and grew and succeeded.

It made perfect sense that Fred would own her home in the end. Fred and his variety were taking over the world. Not that he was a bad person or that it was a bad thing, Annie reminded herself. He was just so much stronger, more resilient, and resistant to disease and drought conditions. A hardy species, like those morning glories he had planted beside the house that rose up now into wild and tangled vines while everything around them appeared strangled or dead. They bloomed when all else withered.

By the end of that hot and fecund afternoon, Annie had agreed to sell her parents' home to Fred Marcatelli. He would finally move up to the hill and Annie and her parents would be paid a weak, though not humiliating, price. Fred insisted they shake on it. Then he kissed her harder on the lips and for once seemed to notice that she did not kiss him back.

"I hope this doesn't complicate things between us too much," he said.

Now Annie was the one to laugh.

"I know you've been preoccupied and everything with your folks," he said. "I didn't want to disturb you. I'm sorry they're doing so badly. I figured you'd call, but you never did."

"I know, Fred, I just—" she began, but he interrupted her.

His words came tumbling out. "I want you to know I met someone at the office. She used to work for my uncle but quit when she had kids, before her divorce. Now her youngest is going into kindergarten—what a doll baby that little girl is, you should see her—and Victoria needed a job. Vicky's her name. I think she's into me, but I got to be clear I'm available, you know, like you and me are over, right? I mean I know we are, but just making sure, in case she wants to get serious."

Annie wondered if she had ever seen Fred so flustered or unsure before. Maybe he'd finally met his match in this woman Victoria who clearly had him in knots. He sounded as if he needed Annie's approval, and so she gave it with a smile that was almost more than she could muster. It seemed to make him happy and set him free.

"All right, then, Annie. We're good, right?" He offered her the thumbs up and stepped away. "Give your mom a hug for me, and all the best to Mr. James, too. I got to hand it to him—he's really hanging in there."

Fred's car left a ring of black oil on the driveway. But it was his driveway now, or soon would be, Annie told herself—his to fix or stain as he saw fit.

From then on, all communication took place between their brokers. Annie engaged a new one because Babs said it was a conflict of interest for her to sell a house to her cousin. She explained that she needed to stay aboveboard in a business where reputation was everything. The papers to accept Fred's offer arrived and Annie's father signed them with a trembling hand. Everyone knew he didn't have long to live. It wasn't clear if he understood how little they would be getting, or that the money would not go to Annie, but instead to pay the bills that had accumulated and those to come from the retirement home for her mother. He muttered that Annie could enjoy the old homestead now.

"You can love it as we did, my girl," he whispered.

Annie's mother patted her arm and gave her a look, so Annie didn't correct him.

Her mother was Annie's main concern now. The cancer had spread and the chemo was making her sick. Annie missed days of work as she drove her to and from the hospital. At the end of the day, she couldn't bear to leave her mother. Some nights she even slept on the pull out sofa in the cramped apartment living room while her father's nurse had the guest room. Annie just wanted to be around.

On the day of the house closing, her mother threw up repeatedly and seemed incoherent. Fearing dehydration, Annie rushed her to the emergency room. A call came in on her cell phone from the real estate broker, but she couldn't pick it up in the hospital. Later, in a stall in the ladies room, Annie listened to the message.

The deal had gone through. The new broker tried to sound chipper, but it was hard to mask the fact that they had practically given the place away in the end. Annie didn't cry. She carefully folded toilet paper and tucked it into her sleeve for when she might cry. But the tears remained stubborn, even when she stood by the bed where her mother lay unconscious.

A week, two, then a month later, on a bright Saturday in October when her mother had fought her way to a shaky remission and her father continued to barely hold on, Annie drove out to the house in her mother's car, which was now hers. She didn't think about where she was going. The old car just drove out the familiar roads before Annie had a chance to think about it. She pulled up in front and parked like a guest.

The lawn looked terrible. Weeds poked high above the overgrown grass. She walked down the front walk, where random bricks had been pulled up, though Annie couldn't imagine why. She peered in through the small leaded window on the front door. The house remained empty, as stark and forlorn as the final time she had walked through it in July. Then she noticed a bright orange sign taped to the living room window: no doubt, she thought, a town permit that would allow Fred to renovate the old place.

Annie stepped around her mother's rhododendrons and looked more closely at the sign. When she saw the word *Demolition*, she stopped reading. She turned away abruptly and headed down the side path. Out of the corner of her eye, she saw a second identical sign bearing the same word taped to the kitchen door.

She continued around the side of the house and her heart pounded hard. Annie told herself to breathe. To look away. To turn back. Her parents were expecting her at the nursing home and she needed to stay strong for their sakes. She stumbled over bare spots where flagstones had been removed from the path. Why had Fred pulled them up, she suddenly wanted to know with great urgency. And why was he tearing down the house?

Annie tried to control the trembling that had started at the tips of her fingers and rose up her arms and into her shoulders. She stopped on the edge of the grass and stared at the stump of the old oak tree. The tree was gone. Taken down and carted away.

Then, finally, the sobs began. They rose up in her and shook her body from head to toe and there was no stopping them. The wide, pale tree stump glared back at her, the grain inside so light it hurt her eyes with its brightness. A soda can and a balled-up fast-food wrapper had been left behind on the raw wood.

Annie looked up into the shadeless sky that flooded the dry fish pool with sunlight. The pond was empty now, only a mash of decomposed leaves and mud coated the bottom. A dead fish lay near the broken filter that gurgled helplessly with no water to pump. Annie's heart thudded madly and she wiped the tears that kept flowing, although she tried to hold them back. She squeezed her arms around her ribs and told herself to calm down.

Then she turned toward the flowerbed where delphiniums and phlox, bee balm and black-eyed Susans usually bloomed all summer, every summer. Now it lay empty, stripped of anything growing. The area was just a gash of black soil—soil her mother had worked so hard to make rich. The roses had been reduced to stumps, their limbs first cut back to the quick, and some pulled up by the roots.

Deep tire marks cut across the lawn. They led down the slope to a pile of branches and plants, all flung together before the rock wall. Ferns and rhododendrons, azaleas and wildflowers had been tossed like bodies into a

common grave. She followed the tracks and stopped
before the pile that rose taller than her. High at the top
lay branches of laurel, the pink blossom skirts no less
delicate for being hurled onto a garbage heap.

Annie looked down at the ruined, churned-up grass
where she used to lie as a child and as a teenager, and
even more recently. The tire tracks had dug a path
through the soft bed of her past. She hugged her ribs even
tighter, just as her mother had on mornings in summer
when she came in from the yard and gave Annie a squeeze
and a happy kiss, clearly pleased with herself, and with
life, and all that lay ahead. Annie had felt that way, too:
hopeful and ready, just because she was her mother's
daughter in her mother's garden.

Annie understood she would have to look elsewhere
from now on to find such beauty and joy. She hoped she
had it in her to do so. She found it hard to believe that
Freddie Marcatelli, of all people, had been the one to force
her to leave—that Freddie Marcatelli had pushed her out
and onward with her life—but he had. She knew she
would never want to speak to him again when they saw
each other around town or at the school. Annie found
herself imagining telling him just how much she despised
him, really loathed him. But also, she knew she owed him
her miserable, furious gratitude.

She touched her own damp neck and brought her
forearm up to meet her lips. She tasted the saltiness there.
It was the same as her mother's skin after working in the
yard. A bitter, sweet taste and scent that made Annie weak
with memory. The sunlight, stark now with no veil of
trees to filter though, struck her cheeks. The last light of
Indian summer burnished her. She squinted through
moist lashes, searching, digging, tilling the garden of what
had been and was no more.

Shelf Life of Happiness

G loria kissed Nathan for the first time in the elevator
as they left work to meet their spouses at a Middle
Eastern place downtown. It wasn't passionate or long,
but instead struck him as defiant. She was trying to rule
out the possibility of their love by finally acting on it, a
paradox he instinctively understood. Love required just
such transpositions.

At the restaurant, Gloria swooped in on her husband,
Bill, adjusted his collar and patted down his unkempt hair.
He brushed her hand aside and gave her a deep kiss.
Nathan's wife, Melissa, returned from the ladies' room
and gave him a peck on the cheek and he delicately
brushed his lips against hers.

A belly-dancing waitress appeared and handed them
menus. She undulated as she filled their water glasses and
Nathan noticed beads of sweat in her cleavage. Sheer
lavender sleeves billowed near his cheek and one of her
sequins lightly pricked his arm. In that moment, he sensed
Gloria's gaze from across the table flaming around him.
He worried Melissa could tell he was caught by that look.
Nathan felt suspended in air, a show dog frozen mid-
leap. It occurred to him he had been there before.

Ten years earlier, he had visited Gloria's college dorm room and sat on her single bed. He was too shy to look directly at her, but instead studied her perfectly painted toenails. As she prattled on about her father, the famous novelist, Nathan laughed with nervous joy: he, Nathan Ripley, was sitting on Gloria Broadhurst's bed. When he made himself come to and followed her words, he was surprised to realize that she didn't grasp that the Old Lion, as her father was called, was considered passé, his moment in the sun long over.

"I bet you're every bit as good a writer as your old man," he tossed out, a back-handed compliment if he'd ever given one.

Gloria didn't hear it that way. She reached across and took Nathan's hands in hers and her eyes became moist. "No," she said. "*You're* the writer. You're the one who's got it."

She had no idea of her impact on someone like him, an orthodontist's son from New Jersey. All he had ever done was read books and scribble in journals. But after hearing Gloria's pronouncement and looking into her convincing eyes, Nathan saw the possibility, the hope, that he was becoming the man he wanted most to become.

The waitress set down dishes that filled the air with heady aromas. As the friends paused in conversation to admire the food, Nathan felt something press urgently against his ankle and he shifted his foot away from Gloria's advancing boot.

In the autumn after college, she had taken an entry-level editorial job at her father's publisher and had then gotten Nathan an interview for a proofreader spot there as well. When the elevator returned him to the lobby after the interview, Gloria stood waiting for him in her pumps and suit, already looking like the publishing professional she would become. She held her thumbs up, the polish flashing, eyebrows raised high, until Nathan nodded shyly that, yes, he'd been offered the job. She rushed toward him, her heels clacking on the marble, and hugged him so hard he stumbled backwards.

But Gloria caught him, put her arm into his, and marched him outside. Rush-hour traffic was backed up on Fifth Avenue, red brake lights glaring in the dusk. As they wove through the crowded sidewalk, she carried on about their plans. They were going to take the book world, and by extension the city, and even the country, by storm. He would write great books and she would see to it that they were published, making her own reputation in the process. When Gloria finally stopped talking, Nathan looked at her and saw that her cheeks were flushed and she looked painfully pretty. He knew what he would remember from that day: a bigger, brighter, more successful version of himself there, reflected back at him from her eyes. It lasted for only a moment, but would sustain Nathan for years.

Now Gloria set down her fork laden with spicy food and announced, "Bill and I have become boring. I always said shoot me if I become boring. I think the time has come."

Bill pointed a finger at his wife's temple and cocked his thumb. Then he let his hand fall heavily to her shoulder and tugged gently on a strand of her fallen hair.

"Some people seem willing to do anything to be happy, even if it means becoming colossally dull," Gloria continued. "But everyone knows it's fleeting. There's always a shelf life of happiness."

Melissa appeared to consider the question, though Nathan hoped not too hard.

Gloria shifted towards him, startling him away from his wife as she often did. "Nathan understands what I mean," she said. "As a writer, he grasps the need to reinvent ourselves."

Nathan lifted his glass and offered his own pronouncement. "Gloria, I believe you will never have a boring life. You will throw parties and have interesting friends and do brilliant things and, in the end, you will be—"

"Yes?" She leaned closer.

"Very, very happy."

She gave a satisfied smile and Bill raised his beer to Nathan. That's when he felt the pressure against his ankle again. Only this time he didn't move. It was the toe of Gloria's sapphire-blue alligator cowboy boot, the ones her father had brought back from Havana their senior year in college. It was making its way up his pant leg, and Nathan, in deference to something so beyond him as that outrageous boot and all it stood for, let it.

When they got back to their apartment, Melissa went to the bedroom to change while Nathan took out the cat food. Their longhaired Persian rubbed against his legs and purred so loudly he could hardly hear Melissa's voice from the bedroom. He set down the cat bowl, washed his hands, and went to his wife.

"Do you think she's all right?" she asked.

"She's fine. She was just hungry."

"Not the cat. Here, help me."

Nathan squeezed between the bed and dresser and began undoing the buttons on the back of Melissa's dress.

"Gloria."

Nathan stopped unbuttoning.

"She seemed strange tonight. You think she's sick or something? She looked pale."

Nathan recalled Gloria on the subway downtown, sweat glistening on her forehead and gathering in the dip above her top lip. "I think she's OK."

"Go on, finish me. It astounds me that men can't think and do at the same time."

Nathan went back to fiddling with the buttons.

"She and Bill really don't seem happy."

Nathan grunted in agreement. Then he turned his wife around and lifted her dress over her head. She made a soft sound and he began to kiss her.

Melissa pulled back. "But you should check on her. You were her friend first."

Nathan's hands stopped what they had started.

"She'll talk to you," Melissa insisted. "She adores you."

Nathan did his best to ignore his wife's words and let his own fast-beating heart decide what to do next.

"Sorry we're late," Nathan said as he and Melissa joined Gloria and Bill at the Village Vanguard later that same evening.

"We got a little distracted," Melissa added, looking down and hiding a smile. "Still newlyweds, I guess."

Gloria didn't seem to notice. She took Melissa's elbow and steered her toward the bar as Nathan and Bill edged closer to the stage.

"I hear Casey's still in top form," Bill said, belching quietly into his fist. "What an icon. The man casts a serious shadow."

"If I were a blues guitarist, I'd just give it up," Nathan said. "Why bother, when old guys like Casey are around? There's no competing with the masters."

"It's all right, buddy." Bill squeezed Nathan's shoulder. "Not everyone can be a Hemingway, am I right?"

Nathan suddenly wished he were home in bed with his cat and a heavy book on his chest. The wives returned and Melissa handed him a glass of wine, which he drank too quickly. Gloria, he noticed, wasn't drinking. Her cheeks looked flushed, as did the pink skin above the V of her sweater where freckles still suggested the tan she somehow managed to keep year round. Nathan edged closer to Melissa and breathed in the sweet smell of her. He knew it wasn't fair to count on his wife to save him from his own wayward feelings, but there it was.

Bill pointed his beer at Nathan and Melissa and said, "They look happy."

Melissa tried to hide her smile again and Nathan squeezed her to his side. As he did, he noticed a wash of sadness pass over Gloria's eyes. Bill must have seen it, too. He pulled her toward him with his thick arms. Their hug seemed to rescue Gloria from whatever forlorn cul de sac she had taken herself down. She tipped her neck back and searched for Bill's lips with her own.

Nathan said he needed another glass of wine and headed off toward the bar. The crowd pressed in and he worried he might faint. He wanted a waitress to take pity on him and bring him more alcohol and while she was at it untangle him from the knot of his own desires. Then applause broke out and the crowd swelled forward to see Casey.

Nathan started back toward the stage, but Gloria appeared suddenly at his side. She took hold of his sleeve and pulled him into the hall next to the restrooms and the pay phone. With his back jammed against the black receiver, her lips reached up to his and this time the kiss was full on and complete. Nathan's fingers touched her cheeks and his temples throbbed with panic: about Melissa, but also himself, and Gloria, not to mention Bill, twice his size, then Melissa again.

They pulled apart. Even in the dim light of the overhead bulb, Gloria's blue eyes pierced him, pinning him writhing now to the wall. The bite of ammonia wafted from the bathroom, and her face was beautiful, though blank and uncomprehending.

"It's not like I never thought about this—" he said.

"Me neither," she said.

"I mean, I did," he tried to clarify. "Never mind," he added. "But you never did?"

Gloria's fingertips traveled the curve of his collarbone and she shook her head. He studied the jagged darkness of her part where the blond stopped and her true color showed. Who was she to him, he asked himself for the thousandth time? But having no answer, he pushed off, took Gloria by the hand, and led her back through the swaying crowd. With nothing but the kiss to regret, he didn't look back or allow himself to consider more. They returned to Bill and Melissa and listened to the best blues in New York, or maybe the world.

The next day's *Village Voice* proclaimed Casey a master. The critic gushed that the old man had as much grace in his left pinkie as the rest of the city had in its entirety. Nathan thought that was a bit hard on the rest of us, although he realized he was in no position to argue. He'd been awake until dawn again. His partially written novel was weighing on him, and images of Gloria pulsed through his brain. Grace was a concept he hardly needed reminding of five days before Christmas with Melissa beside him.

They took a New Jersey Transit bus back into the city at the end of Christmas Day. On the rack overhead, they had stuffed shopping bags full of gifts and turkey leftovers. Nathan undid his belt a notch and Melissa rested her head on his shoulder and dozed. Her parents had outdone themselves, giving them a casserole, a serving platter, and an ice bucket, envisioning them hosting their friends with gin and tonics and pot roast, as they had when they were first married. Nathan felt grateful to be so encumbered. His in-laws asked very little of him, just that Melissa remain happy, which, mostly due to her own good disposition, she managed much of the time. Now, in the green glow of the bus lights, she snored softly into his lapel. He couldn't have felt more contented, and congratulated himself on not having thought of Gloria once all day.

The phone rang at two that morning and Nathan grabbed it from the cradle. Melissa rolled over in her sleep as he whispered a sharp hello into the receiver, preparing to punish the caller who had dialed the wrong number. It was bad enough to be sleepless, but worse to be caught at it. When he heard the reply, he spoke no less harshly.

"You can't call me in the middle of the night."

Nathan shifted the cat on the comforter, climbed out of bed, and pulled the phone as far as it would reach. With the bathroom door shut behind him, he lowered the lid and sat.

Gloria spoke through tears. "Bill's furious. He's absolutely livid."

More crying, which Nathan ignored, his heart freezing up. She couldn't have told Bill. Nathan pulled the neck of his t-shirt away from his throat. Steam came in repeated bursts from the vertical pipe beside the toilet: a single iron rod, paint peeling in little squares, terribly hot to the touch. Nathan studied the menacing thing.

"He was blind drunk," Gloria said. "Maybe he won't remember it in the morning."

"What would he remember?" Nathan put his hand up beside the pipe and dared himself to touch it.

"The man prefers blindness. Don't you find that most people prefer blindness?"

Nathan flicked off a square of peeling paint and snatched his finger away, the burn registering on the tip.

"I've tried to be honest with him," Gloria continued. "I've never pretended to be an angel."

Nathan placed his palm around the pipe and gently squeezed. It took a moment for the pain to sear into him.

"What did you tell him, Gloria?" he asked through gritted teeth.

"It's a long story. You, of all people, know what a long story it is. Can I see you in the morning? I *need* to see you."

So this is how it happens, Nathan thought, releasing his hand. The meetings. The urgency. The need. The throbbing sensation traveled all the way to his shoulder. He held his red palm up before him in the dim light. They made a plan and Nathan hung up quickly, his whole body registering the pain now and writhing with it. He hurried to the sink and turned on the cold water and thrust his hand under.

Nathan had agreed to meet Gloria in Father Demo Square, a triangle of concrete at an intersection in the West Village with a few leafless trees and wooden benches. He stood in the empty island and noticed the sign over the pizza place on the corner. He had walked past it several times a day for three years and had never before read the name of the joint. Nathan chided himself for being oblivious to what was right in front of his eyes.

Melissa had been filling the tub with bubble bath when she asked him where he was going. Grateful for the loud rush of water to drown out the fear in his voice, Nathan shouted back that he still had a Christmas surprise in store for her. He would be back soon. But his wife hadn't been content to leave it at that. She rose from the tub and shook off the water then dashed out into the kitchen, soap foam trailing behind her, as naked as he had ever seen her. She planted a quick, tart, promising kiss on his lips. He told himself to never forget that kiss and the sight of her lovely, lithe body as she turned and slipped back into the bath. Never forget the delicate trail of soap foam he stepped over on his way out the door to ruin his marriage.

From his seat on a bench, Nathan watched Gloria cut across Sixth Avenue, her winter coat flapping open to expose an oversized sweatshirt and flannel pajama bottoms tucked into rain boots. Her hair was up in a utilitarian bun and she wore no make-up, something that would attract no notice on Melissa, but on Gloria made her eyes appear pinched and pale. They looked down on him now, not with their iridescent blue brightness, but with a dull, gray light, as if snow were on her personal horizon.

Nathan stood and assumed they would hug, maybe even kiss, but Gloria slipped past him and flopped onto the bench. Noticing her peeling nail polish as she ran a hand through disheveled hair, Nathan felt sorry for her. Periodically, over the years, he had felt that way. But then some great good luck would appear in Gloria's life: an invitation to the Oscars from an old Hollywood friend, an offer to speak about her father's literary legacy at a conference in Paris, a personal essay accepted by the *Times* on traveling with your cat, because it wasn't any cat, but Gloria Broadhurst's cat. Nathan scolded himself. Although he suspected that she might eventually blow through several marriages, or become renowned in publishing circles not always for the right reasons, Gloria would never be the one with the sorry life.

"Sit," she said, patting the bench with a bare hand. "I need to talk to you."

Nathan thrust his gloves deeper into his pockets and sat. "You should button your coat if you're cold."

She nodded, but didn't move to do so. Two elderly women crossed the park, their thick bodies bundled against the weather and their hands moving as they talked.

"Bill's done with me."

Nathan let out a long, white breath and braced himself for what would come next. He tried to bear it, but couldn't and had to speak up.

"I don't think you should have told him. We've got"— his voice slid downward—"our lives to think about . . . our marriages."

Gloria squinted at him in the morning light. As Nathan steeled himself to insist that she—but Gloria's chilly index finger reached across and pressed against his lips before he could open them to speak again. It stayed there as he went quiet. Nathan looked at her and saw a glint of pity cross her face. It came and went briefly, though he was certain he had seen it.

"Oh, Nathan," she said and let her hand drop to her lap. "It's not you. It's never been you." She gazed at the blur of traffic going by. "I needed to talk. I can always count on you. You're such a good friend."

He felt the cold bench under him, the slats of icy wood against his back. All of him, all of a sudden, chilled and solid. The stoplight changed as yellow cabs hurtled up the avenue and Gloria continued.

"I thought my own husband would want to know why I've been feeling so lousy. When Melissa's sick you give a shit, don't you?"

Nathan leaned forward, his elbows on his knees as he let her words sink in. *Oh, Nathan. It's never been you.* How had he ever thought otherwise? He had known the truth, but had written a different version in his own mind. Now he studied the side of Gloria's face and noticed a dark mole just below the ear, the delicacy of her features not lost on him, but also no longer enticing him to reach out and touch her or define them with words. He needed to let go of the mystery of her, the complete unknowableness of Gloria Broadhurst. It had always been as pointless as clutching at a puff of air and, had he ever succeeded, would have been just about as rewarding.

He let out a slight laugh and leaned back and stretched out his arms, more light-hearted than he'd felt in some time. Gloria's red-rimmed eyes gazed at the street, and Nathan decided in that moment that he would remain her confidant for life, the role, he now understood, she had assigned to him so many years before. Perhaps Melissa had been right and Gloria really was sick, maybe even with something terrible like breast cancer, or a creeping illness like MS or leukemia. Her finger on his lips had dammed up the possibility of their love, but that made sense if her illness was the bigger, truer story. He felt enormous relief and grateful to her for stopping him before he unspooled completely in her presence. He wouldn't act the fool any longer. He would help her through her difficult time ahead. He would be her friend.

"You can tell me," he said, feeling bolstered by his own sincerity. "I want to know everything."

A flock of pigeons circled and landed on the ground before them.

"I've been such an idiot," she said. "You were always so solid and good. I should have married someone like you instead." She flung her arms toward the pigeons.

Nathan watched the bobbing, anxious swarm of birds scatter. They lifted off from the ground in a blanket of movement, but then settled quickly again in the same place. Like the birds, he did his best to take things in stride.

"You know, I think you're the best man I've ever known," she said, "besides my father."

Nathan couldn't help smiling now. Married four times, Gloria's father had been a renowned philanderer.

"You're better than the rest of them. Really, you are. Better than my own damned husband, anyway." She stomped her foot for emphasis and the pigeons shot off again.

This time the birds rose to the telephone wires in a flutter of flapping wings and cooing complaints. Nathan followed them with his eyes. Though he felt quite certain he would be happy with Melissa for many years to come, he knew that his memory of this cold, damp morning in the West Village would stay with him for just as long. This would forever be the morning when he let go of his hope of being the kind of man who could attain a woman like Gloria. He knew now who he was and who he would continue to be: a regular guy who loved his wife.

"Remember last August when I went down to Key West?" Gloria asked.

Nathan shook his head.

"It was just a quick trip. I may not even have mentioned it. And I wouldn't have thought twice about it until the doctor pressed me to be precise. Anyway, this old friend of Papa's was down there."

Nathan sat forward on the bench. "Papa?"

"He's the nephew of an old family friend, actually."

"But which Papa?"

"What do you mean?"

"You said Key West."

"Oh, for God's sake, Nathan." Gloria laughed and looked pretty again and suddenly flush with worlds he would never know. "Not *that* Papa. Of course my father and he were great friends, old drinking buddies. They sparred all the time about writing. That's what you writers do, but that's not what this is about. You need to let it go. Not everything comes back to writing and books and your big, manly ambitions. Sometimes, there's just life."

Nathan laughed a little, too, and released her hand. But instead of dismissing the thought, her words struck him as a challenge and he felt surer than ever of what he wanted. By writing in the evenings and in the hours before work, he would finally finish his first novel. He felt certain it would be published and then more novels would follow after that. He would do it with or without Gloria Broadhurst's enthusiasm and connections. He could even picture future dedication pages, each to Melissa, and someday to their children as well. Although he would never mention Gloria in his books, he would write because of her, but not for her.

Gloria had started up talking again and he forced himself to listen more attentively. Apparently, she hadn't seen this guy since they were children together down in Key West. Neither of them had planned it. No one could plan such a thing. It was passion. Nothing had mattered to them in that moment but the moment. As she carried on, Nathan began to hate this stranger, the nephew of her father's friend who had succeeded in winning Gloria when he had not. Nathan hated her father, too, for his machismo and lasting success and for being the kind of man and writer that Nathan would never be. For that matter, he hated old Papa himself because it all came back to him and the fucking long shadow he cast over lesser writers, men who sweated over their versions of the blues and had wives they returned to at the end of the day.

"It's high time we grew up, isn't it, Nathan?" Gloria was saying. "This baby is exactly what I needed."

He looked across at the pizza place and told himself to memorize the shiny black lettering above the door and the weather that day and Gloria's voice, for he knew each detail was already slipping away into the past. But it was all right because he would capture it, or something like it, in his own words, and that would have to be enough.

"Now you understand why I had to see you," she said and reached for his hand again. "We're such old friends. I wanted you to know why I've been acting so crazy. I've been terribly unhappy." She leaned into him and offered a sorrowful smile. "But when it comes down to it, who *is* happy these days, that's what I want to know? Really. Tell me. Who is?"

Nathan put his arm around Gloria Broadhurst's shoulder. It didn't matter who saw them now, what neighbors or strangers. It didn't matter what he brought home to Melissa that morning: a single rose from the green grocer's, a cream tart from the patisserie around the corner, or a simple loaf of fresh baked bread.

All he wanted was to step inside his steamy apartment and see his wife in her bathrobe, water beading at the nape of her neck and in the tender hollows of her collarbone. And in a corner of their cramped living room, his typewriter sat waiting for him on a desk made of a hollow door and milk crates. Nathan knew the answer to Gloria's question, although he didn't dare say it aloud for fear it might disappear on a cloud of moist breath and air.

Acknowledgments

I'm grateful to the following journals for first publishing these stories: *The Baltimore Review* for "New Year's Day"; *Tampa Review* for "White Dog"; *Failbetter* for "Redbone"; *Prime Number Magazine* for "Best Man" and "Easter Morning"; *SheBooks* for "Her Mother's Garden"; *Abundant Grace, an Anthology of Women Writers,* edited by Richard Peabody, for "Crying in Italian," formerly "The Lemon Man"; and *Pangyrus* for "An Awesome Gap."

Rosemary Ahern, Gigi Amateau, Nathan Long, Pamela Painter, Zoe Rosenfeld, Jon Sealy, Mollie Sherry, Patty Smith, and others helped me greatly by reading early drafts of these stories. Additional generous fellow writers—Margaret Grant, Bonnie Waltch, Jodi Paloni, Janyce Stefan-Cole, Cliff Garstang, Leslie Pietrzyk, and Mary Akers—helped bring this project across the finish line. And great thanks also to Joan Silber, Jim Shepard, Jenny Boylan, Steve Yarbrough, and Kelly Luce—all of whose work I greatly admire—for generously reading and supporting this collection.

I so appreciate the expertise of Caitlin Hamilton Summie for her excellent efforts on publicity; and the talented designer and artist, and dear friend, Margaret Buchanan, for her beautiful cover. Most of all, my thanks goes to Kevin Morgan Watson for accepting this collection and for his insightful editing, and for welcoming me into the Press 53 family.

Kate Davis and Julie Heffernan inspire me with their unflagging commitment to their art. And, of course, as always, this is for John Ravenal, who makes my writing and life better by the day.

Cover designer Margaret Buchanan is an award-winning graphic designer and head of Buchanan Design, which she founded in 1989. She is a painter, photographer, and book artist. Her work has been exhibited nationally and is represented in numerous private collections, including the Federal Reserve Bank of Richmond, Bank of America, Media General, and the Virginia Commonwealth University Medical Center. Her hand-built, limited-edition book, *First Impression: A China Diary*, is part of the Columbia University Rare Book and Manuscript Library.

Virginia Pye is the author of two award-winning novels, *Dreams of the Red Phoenix* and *River of Dust*. Her stories, essays, and interviews have appeared in *The North American Review*, *The Baltimore Review*, *Literary Hub*, *The New York Times*, *The Rumpus*, *Huffington Post* and elsewhere. She lived in Richmond, Virginia, for many years and now lives in Cambridge, Massachusetts.

CPSIA information can be obtained
at www.ICGtesting.com
Printed in the USA
BVHW031230200519
548789BV00012B/1308/P